Twisted Pulses

A Horror Collection

By Leigh Foley

AF278892

This is a work of fiction. Names, characters, organizations, places, events, and incidents are either products of the author's imagination or are used fictitiously.

Text copyright © 2026 Leigh Foley

All rights reserved. No part of this book may be reproduced, or stored in a retrieval system, or transmitted in any form or by any means, electronic, mechanical, photocopying, recording, or otherwise, without express written permission of the publisher.

Portions of this collection were previously published. The versions contained in this volume have been revised and edited by the author.

ISBN-13: 978-0-9967897-4-5

Horror, horror everywhere,
let's all have a read.

Twisted Pulses is a horror collection that spans styles,
themes, and fears.
Buckle up, buttercup, and prepare for discomfort.

Stories

JAM

Throat raw from ceaseless
screams. Voice lost in an ocean
of hushed negligence.

The pinprick of a
shadow drags behind listless,
cement-heavy steps.

Nothing, not even
the sturdiest promises,
can endure this dread.

∞∞∞∞

Peel the skin. Flay the
flesh. Dissect the electric
pulse between heart beats.

∞∞∞∞

Canned

My mother loved me, but she lived for my summer trips to Aunt Evelyn and Uncle Garret's farm. They were her childfree break, her chance to experience life without someone to look after. For me, the trips were a way to escape the weight of her constant worrying. I recognized this even as a young child. A month apart gave us the space we needed from each other. It was enough of a break to make the rest of the year bearable.

My father left when I was a few days old, so my visits started when I was just a toddler. I was old enough to walk but too young to form complete sentences the first time I went. I basically grew up on my aunt and uncle's farm, learning to enjoy the outdoors while gaining responsibility by caring for the animals living on their acres.

At home, I wasn't allowed to get dirty or look unkempt. Momma was very strict about my upbringing and didn't want the neighbors looking down on her for any reason. Being a single mom meant she put extra pressure on herself to be the best parent she could. Part of that was ensuring I looked well taken care of at all times. I didn't mind being clean, but the pressure to look perfect got on my nerves. Momma was constantly on my tail, nagging me to scrub under my fingernails or brush my hair. Her pestering annoyed my inner spirit, the one who preferred a thick layer of dirt.

During my summer visits to the farm, I was free to be a wild child, to roll in the mud with the dogs or jump on the fence posts with the chickens. I showered in the hose and only came inside when I heard my aunt calling for dinner. It was glorious just to be, to bask in the earthy smells that coated my clothes and skin.

During the first ten years of visits, my uncle was a loving part of each stay. Every morning, when he got up to milk the cows and gather eggs from the coop, he stopped in my room to rustle me awake.

"Pssst. Sweet pea." He'd gently shake my shoulder. "The sun's a rising and so should we. Get on up and help your Uncle Garret with his chores. They get done much faster when my wrangler-in-training is there."

"Yes, sir." I bounced out of bed, ready to take on the day. My boots and socks were stored near the foot of the bed for easy access, and I put them on with haste. "Can I milk Bailey today? Please, Uncle Garret. She's my favorite."

"Of course, sugar. I think you're big enough to do it all by yourself. But let's get moving before your auntie gets on our tails! You know she wants fresh milk before she starts cooking."

I'd grab his hand, and we'd walk to the barn together, telling jokes as we went.

"How many tickles does it take to make an octopus laugh?" I asked, trying hard to hold my own giggles inside.

He'd wrinkle his brow. "Hmmmmm . . . I'm not sure I've ever met an octopus as ticklish as you, and it only takes one good tickle to make you laugh." He reached over, finding the spot on the side of my ribs that made me squeal in delight. After a moment of merriment, he answered, "See? One tickle. That must be the right answer."

A laugh escaped my throat, and I shook my head after it settled. "Nope. It's ten tickles, Uncle Garret! Get it? Tentacles?"

His hearty chuckle rang through the barn, dancing around until it dissipated into the dusty air. I didn't think my smile could get any bigger, but somehow it always grew at the sound of his laughter.

Every day, he'd say the same thing. His twinkling eyes would fix on me, a spark of seriousness shining through. "You're pretty funny, short stuff. Keep it up. A good sense of humor will get you through anything. Even these chores we're about to do."

But I never saw our morning activities as chores. They were just something we did to gather ingredients for breakfast. They served a purpose, and a fun one at that. Giggling with my uncle added to the charm.

I associated chore time with making my bed, folding the laundry, and grocery shopping with Momma back home. I did those out of obligation and a sense of duty. Momma needed help, so I helped. But Uncle Garret never *needed* assistance. He enjoyed my company, and I enjoyed his. Together, our mornings were the highlight of my day.

Collecting breakfast ingredients wasn't the only way I helped around the farm. My aunt and uncle kept a large garden; rows and rows of plants growing on a sloping field. The greenery supplied them with fresh fruits and vegetables throughout the harvest season and preserved goods the rest of the year. I loved running between the rows of leafy vegetables and colorful fruits. It was magical knowing the plants had grown from seed and that they would feed my aunt and uncle for the entire year.

Life was straightforward on the farm. You raised your own food and didn't have to depend on grocery stores to survive. It was so different from life in the city. The farm's slow pace and charming simplicity eased my young mind of the anxiety I brought from home.

When I was eleven, Uncle Garret had an accident. One moment, he was stacking feed bags on the barn's second story, and the next, he became a crumpled heap on the packed earth below. The fall wasn't even that high, but it was enough to deliver a wallop.

Human beings are tough, and no one was tougher than my uncle. His humor didn't mean that he was weak in any way. I'd seen him face down a snarling wolf when it attempted to steal away a newly birthed foal. And that was just one example of his strength. There were plenty more.

On Momma's and my drive to the farm, I clung to stories of people who had survived tumbles from penthouse apartments. I told myself that if a normal person could live after plummeting onto a concrete sidewalk, my tough-as-nails uncle could handle a fall from just 20 feet. I knew this minor accident wasn't going to be his demise.

But it was.

While Aunt Evelyn, Momma, and I sat by his side, Uncle Garret left the earthly realm. His eyes never opened. There were no loving last words or reassuring hugs. My uncle just blinked out of existence after a shuddering exhale.

The keening wail that leapt from my aunt's throat summed up the feelings in the room. Her wail saturated the atmosphere, making it heavy with heartbreak. Grief dragged us all down.

Eventually, Momma shook off her sorrow and summoned the doctor to report the passing. I'm unsure how much time passed before she gathered the strength to stumble into the living room to make the call. Time stopped mattering by that point. If there was any measure of the day draining by, it was counted in tears rather than seconds. Thousands of droplets journeyed from my eyes to the tan sheet covering my uncle, staining the fabric with their aquatic misery.

Dr. Welling arrived at the house after three hundred tears. It took fifty more for him to certify the death, and twenty more to express his condolences. With a bow of his head, the doctor left us alone with our sorrow.

In the small country town that my aunt and uncle lived in, the process of death was handled informally. Families buried their own, which meant funeral homes were not a thriving business in the area. The closest hospital was a two-hour drive away, so the local doctor was the person families summoned when a relative was anything from ill to catatonic.

Dr. Welling knew my aunt and uncle, knew they were good people, and knew that no foul play caused my uncle's death. He was simply called as a formality, and his quick departure meant he understood this completely. He left Auntie Evelyn alone, so she could prepare the body.

Momma and I stayed on the farm for a week, comforting my aunt as best we could. Twenty years of marriage had forged a bond that had been erased by an unexpected misstep. Something so ordinary stole away the person my aunt loved most in this world. It was unfair and she knew it, but processing her anguish was less simple. Crying helped. Screaming did as well. But neither of those things made up for her loneliness. Or the lips that would never again receive a good morning kiss. Or the hands that would never again feel the gentle pat that meant *I love you.* The little acts representing the connection between my aunt and uncle were the things she would miss most.

Funeral arrangements were kept to a minimum. While Uncle Garret was well-liked, he wasn't a frivolous man. Drawing attention to himself was never something he did in life, and we kept this in mind when we planned the public acknowledgement of his death. A simple pine casket and a memorial picture were the only items decorating the front parlor the day of his funeral. I made a few dozen of Aunt Evelyn's shortbread cookies, and set out a pitcher of lemonade, both Uncle Garret's favorites. But besides those small touches, Momma and I left the house intact.

As guests streamed by the memorial, Aunt Evelyn greeted them mechanically, nodding in response to condolences but never fully connecting with the words. Her eyes were bloodshot, and she had lost enough weight to look sickly.

"Momma," I whispered.

"Keep your voice down, Sara," she hissed.

"I'm sorry. I'm trying to be quiet. It's just that Aunt Evelyn doesn't look so good. Do you think she's going to be okay?"

Her no-nonsense glare softened as she answered. "Sweetheart, it might take some time for your aunt to be okay. She lost someone she loved dearly, and that takes a lot out of a person. It's very nice of you to be worried, but right now, we need to give Evelyn space and let her grieve the way she sees fit. Do you understand?"

I nodded. "I do, Momma. I'm just so sad for her."

She reached over and squeezed my shoulder. "I know you are. And I am, too. But we'll make sure that Evelyn gets through this when she's ready. My brother would expect nothing less from us."

And I was prepared to give Aunt Evelyn as much time as she needed. For me, that meant not going to the farm for my yearly visit, which was scheduled only two months after my uncle's death. If my aunt needed space and time, I was going to give it to her. It was the right thing to do.

But that's not what ended up happening. At Aunt Evelyn's request, I went to her house that summer, and every summer thereafter. When I arrived for my first stay, my aunt's demeanor was surprisingly, almost unnaturally, chipper for a recent widow. I took it as a sign that she was coping well with my uncle's death.

Boy, was I wrong.

This last summer, five years after my uncle's passing, was the first summer I grew uneasy at the farm. Everything started out normally enough, but it progressed from normal to strange very quickly.

My aunt had hired someone to help with the chores after Uncle Garret's death, but each year when I came to visit the farm, the ranch hand took a three-week vacation. During my stays, it was just me and Aunt Evelyn taking care of the property.

Every morning, just like in the earlier years, I would gather eggs and milk for Aunt Evelyn. She'd whip everything into fluffy omelets, and I would gorge myself before heading out to collect whatever fruits and vegetables my aunt needed for cooking or canning. It was hard work, but I loved it.

When Uncle Garret was alive, I occasionally helped my aunt prepare dinner. The two of us would wear matching aprons, and laugh while we chopped, sautéed, and baked homemade deliciousness. Each meal came out smelling as good as it tasted. Auntie Evelyn said everything was yummy because of the love that went into making it. A cheesy sentiment, sure, but I treasured those times with her. They reminded me of everything wholesome at the farm.

But, for the past five years, I hadn't been allowed to help with mealtime preparations. There hadn't been an explanation for the sudden halting of our cooking duo, but I felt like it had something to do with the grief process. Maybe Aunt Evelyn associated cooking with Uncle Garret, and she wanted to keep it to herself. I wasn't mad about being excluded, I was just happy my aunt was doing well.

During dinner prep-time, Auntie Evelyn would send me outside or to my room, and she would holler my name when everything was ready. "Saraaaaaa, it's dinner time. Come and get it!"

And I *would* come and get it! Each dish my aunt served was hearty and filled with subtle flavors that belied their simple ingredients. She certainly knew what she was doing in the kitchen. Everything she brought to the table was consumed quickly by a growing teenager. I never tasted anything I didn't like at my aunt's house.

That was, never until tonight.

The meal was cornbread, collard greens, and pot roast—a favorite that frequently made its way into the dinner rotation. I was always hungry after a day of farm life, so I greedily piled my plate high and started eating.

The seasoned greens and beef were divine like always. I wolfed down half of each before slopping some strawberry jelly and butter on my cornbread. After the first bite of the muffin, I noticed something was off. It just didn't taste right. There was a rancid, oily flavor I couldn't pinpoint.

I furrowed by brow. "Aunt Evelyn, I think something might be wrong with the bread."

She was chewing a piece of bread as I spoke and didn't seem bothered by what she was eating. After she swallowed, she said, "Are you sure, dear? It tastes fine to me. Why don't you grab another piece?"

I did as my aunt suggested and grabbed a different slice of bread. I slathered a layer of butter on and was about to do the same with the jelly, when a putrid odor wafted up. I raised the jar to my nose in an attempt to verify the source of the smell.

A single whiff was all it took. A sweet, meaty scent barreled its way into my nose. I almost lost the contents of my stomach on top of the table. My dry heaving wouldn't stop even after I jerked the jar away from my face. I kept remembering the cloying, fleshy scent. It had made its way from my nose into my brain, and my mind didn't want to forget the putrescent smell.

I heard my aunt's voice between retches. "Sara! What's happening?! Let's get you to the bathroom."

Cool hands grabbed me by the shoulders, guiding me from my chair to the nearest toilet. I was finally able to release the gorge that had been building since my bite of cornbread. The food exiting my insides didn't smell nearly as bad as the jar of jelly, so I was able to stop purging almost as quickly as it had begun. After a few minutes away from the table, the memory of the jam's scent gradually faded from my memory banks, and for that I was grateful.

Aunt Evelyn's voice grabbed my attention away from the toilet. "Is everything okay? I've never seen food poisoning take hold of someone so fast. Do you think you're stable enough to make it to your room?"

I nodded and we began the journey to my bed. I was able to respond to her first question once I was off my feet and lying down. "I don't think that was food poisoning, Aunt Evelyn. And it wasn't the muffins that had something wrong with them, it was the jelly."

She shook her head. "It couldn't be the jelly. I brought that jar up from storage just this morning. It should be extra fresh."

"But it was! It was rotten! If only you had smelled it." I shuddered when I thought about the overpowering odor. The meaty scent would haunt me.

"Now dear, you're just imagining things. Let's not talk about this anymore. Why don't you close your eyes and get some rest? It will make you feel better." And without waiting for a response, Aunt Evelyn hurried from the room.

I didn't have time to process her strange behavior because my eyes *were* getting heavier by the second. She had been right; some rest might help. I gave in to the drowsiness and fell into a deep sleep without trying too hard.

I'm not sure how much time passed before a creaking noise yanked me from my slumber. When the creaking was followed by a light thump, I knew my bedroom door had just closed. My aunt must have been checking on me.

I raised my hands, stretching the sleepiness out of my body. I felt surprisingly good for having been sick not too long ago. The only symptom that hinted at the earlier food exodus was an extremely parched mouth, but that was nothing a glass of water couldn't fix. I rolled out of bed and made my way toward the kitchen.

Thanks to my nap, my eyes were adjusted to the darkness, and I dodged furniture with ease. The kitchen was at the opposite end of the house, so I passed Aunt Evelyn's room during the trek. The warm glow of light peeked out from underneath her door. I must not have slept for too long if she was still up.

My aunt was the "early to bed, early to rise" type of person. She started preparing feed for the horses and pigs well before sunrise and usually went to bed shortly after dinner. Her schedule was perfectly in-tune to the farm. My sudden illness might have caused a slight interruption to her bedtime routine, but I knew it couldn't be past ten.

I crept by her room, holding my breath to avoid making any noise, and crossed the threshold into the kitchen. There was always a jug of cold water in the refrigerator, waiting to slake the thirst of the parched. I filled and drained two cup-fulls from the container before my mouth returned to a normal state.

Despite my best efforts to be quiet, when I set my cup in the sink, the sound of glass hitting metal rang out through the air. I listened for a few seconds, heart pounding, hoping that my aunt hadn't heard my clumsiness. When nothing but silence met my ears, I assumed I was safe from detection. I silently berated my oafish ways as I headed back to my room.

As I passed the dining room table, my foot kicked a piece of paper. I reached down and snagged the item from the floor. The dark made it difficult to see what I was holding, so I brought the small rectangle close to my face. The object was thicker than paper, more like cardstock, and the phrase *Let's Get Cooking!* was printed in a swirly font at the top. A greasy fingerprint marred one corner, but the ink looked fresh and bright. One of my aunt's recipe cards must have fallen out of its box. I knew she'd hate to lose even a single card, as some of the recipes had been passed down through generations. And while the card appeared newer, I knew the words contained on the sheet were precious to Aunt Evelyn, regardless of age.

From our previous cooking experiences, I knew she kept her recipe box in the basement, next to the storage cellar. Instead of heading back to bed, I walked toward the stairs leading to the lower level.

The basement was never my favorite place to go. When I was younger, I asked my uncle to accompany me whenever my aunt sent me down to grab a can of vegetables or bag of flour. He would hold my hand, wordlessly knowing I needed the comfort, and fill the cool, dry atmosphere with his jovial voice. I hadn't made any journeys into the space since his death, but my unease about the basement still remained. And I had no one to ease my fear. My uncle couldn't help me now.

A few measured breaths gave me the push of courage I needed to open the door at the top of the stairs. My forward momentum was halted by frantic words coming from below me.

"Oh, Garret, I know I've already apologized a hundred times but let me say it again. I'm so sorry I tarnished your memory. I never meant to, and I'll make sure it won't happen again. It's the new recipe that threw me off."

It was Aunt Evelyn. And it sounded like she was talking to Uncle Garret. But of course, that couldn't be right. Maybe I was mistaken. Maybe I imagined hearing my uncle's name.

I listened, paying closer attention to the words.

Her voice was shrill. "I'm glad Sara caught my mistake before I ate anything contaminated. I guess there is that to be grateful for."

Contaminated? Was she talking about tonight's dinner? My aunt didn't use jelly on her toast or biscuits. She preferred them plain. This meant she only canned a few containers each year, just enough for me to slather it on everything I could.

She didn't eat the jelly tonight, only I had. And I paid with an upset stomach.

My aunt continued her harried speech. "I just wish there was more of your flesh to use. Living meat seems to spoil much quicker than the preserved kind."

Flesh? Living meat? I couldn't have heard the words accurately. There *had* to be some sort of mix up. Perhaps I was still feeling sick, and this was a dream.

But it wasn't a dream at all. It was a horrifying reality.

When I descended the stairs, I clearly saw my aunt. There was no dreamlike quality distorting my observation of her naked body. Or the oozing wounds covering her skin. Or the tears streaming down her face as she turned to meet my eyes.

"Sara? Did I wake you? I'm so sorry dear. I was just having a conversation with your uncle. I told him we should keep our voices down, but you know how excitable he gets sometimes."

"Aunt Evelyn, are you okay? You're bleeding everywhere." My gaze moved to the ruby-red puddles under her feet. "You need a doctor!"

She shook her head. "There's no need for that, my dear. Me and Garret are trying to figure out what we can do with my body. We need to make it more compatible with the new process. It's not working right now, but I'm sure we'll figure it out soon. We always do." She swept her arm over the puddle of blood beneath her feet. "We'll have this mess cleaned up in no time. Don't worry at all." Her voice was giddy, filled with an excitement mirrored in her eyes.

Shudders rippled through me. "What process are you talking about? Aunt Evelyn, you're not making any sense."

"When your uncle had his accident, the only way to keep him alive was to consume his earthly flesh. The dream angels told me so." She nodded at her words, clasping her hands hard like she was praying. "I couldn't bear to lose my Garret, so I did what those beautiful, winged creatures told me to do. I preserved my soul mate and picked at his meat, consuming him with every meal." She giggled, sounding young and out of her mind. "Sara, can you believe it? When I added his essence to each bite, he joined me at the table for dinner! That first night we had such a nice conversation. He was pleased with my efforts."

A whistly wail escaped her, and wavered around the basement, drilling into my nerves. Tears poured from her eyes as she continued. "Unfortunately, I ran out of his skin this summer." Sorrow flashed in her eyes, damping the madness. "It lasted so long, Sara. He nourished me through five years. For five years he was with me at the table, sharing in our bounty. I stretched him as far as he would go, using only the tiniest bits in the last few containers, but eventually I had to face the truth."

The smell from dinner tonight made sense. Flesh flavored jam went down my throat when I bit into my meal, and then up my throat when I vomited. And who knows how many times before that my uncle found his way inside my stomach. My legs wobbled and dark splotches burst in my vision. But I couldn't black out. Not in this room.

I started backing out of the room, trying to escape the madness radiating from my aunt while avoiding her notice. But I paused my steps at these words. I couldn't resist finding out more. I needed to know exactly what she'd done, for my own sake.

"What truth, Aunt Evelyn?" I asked, my voice trembling.

She spoke with a conviction only the completely insane can muster. "It was my turn to sacrifice, sweetie. Now that Garret was a part of me, if I consumed my own flesh. I'd be eating my love once again. His body wouldn't just fulfill me once. It would continue to do so as long as I had more to give."

She looked down at her bloody limbs and the chunks of flesh missing from her torso. Bright red oozed from the wounds, trickling to the floor in small rivers. "I can't quite get the process right, though. My flesh isn't taking well to being canned." Her shoulders slumped in defeat.

At that, I started running and didn't stop until I reached the closest neighbor's house. The call I placed to Dr. Welling didn't convey the panic, disgust, and anguish I felt. I was remarkably calm for someone who had just been told that they had been dining on their beloved uncle for the past five years. Maybe I was in shock.

When my aunt was placed in a secure facility, I didn't shed a tear. I'd had some time to process the situation and had realized that the advice my Uncle Garret had given me as a child was perfect for the situation—a good sense of humor will get you through anything.

Instead of crying, I laughed my way through each of my days. My mind kept returning to the silly jokes my uncle and I used to share.

"Hey sweet pea, got any jokes today?"

"I sure do, Uncle Garret! You ready?"

"You know it, kiddo."

"What do you call a teenager who was forced to become a cannibal?"

"I don't know, darling. What do you call them?"

You call them me.

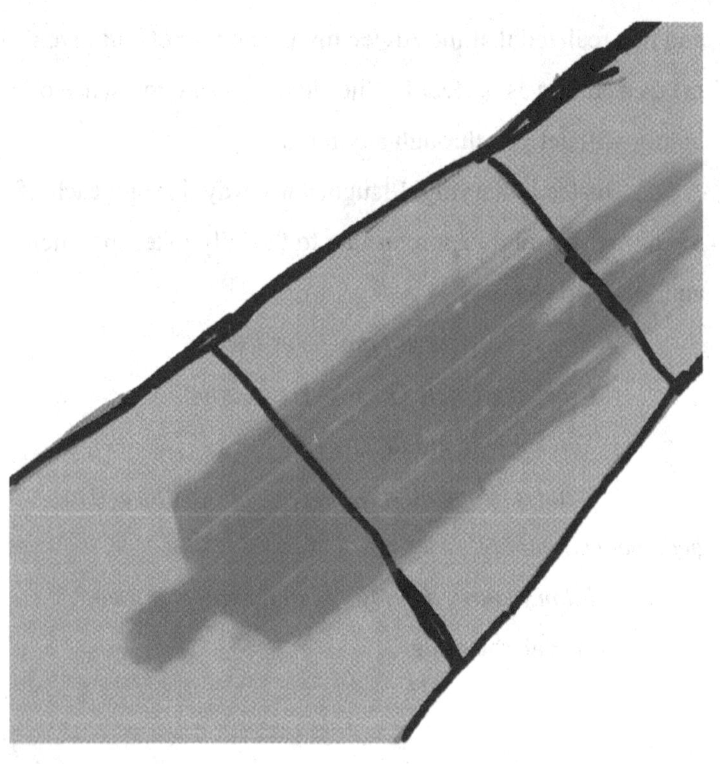

Smirking eyes belie

the concern that drips from lips

pulled into a grin.

∞∞∞∞

Resistance departs

as wasted pleas bounce around

corridors of guilt.

Malleable

Heads don't bounce. You'd think they would because of their spherical shape, but they don't. Trust me. I've witnessed it.

The heat waves rising from the sidewalk snaked around her ankles. Swirling up and down. Undulating.

Generally, the first place I check out on a girl is her tits but sweat dripping down her lithe legs drew my eyes in a southern direction until all I could see were coils of reptilian-like energy twining themselves tighter and tighter.

She seemed unaware. Although my gaze fixated on her feet, I sensed the apathy pouring from her being into the cracked pavement. She never twitched, never flinched, never trembled. Stillness was her state.

It bothered me, her calm. Bothered me so much that my body began to experience empathetic tremors. Wave after wave of spasms rocketed through my muscles. My hands clenched. My toes curled. I was in tune with the pulsed rhythm her scaly beasts were beating.

Her aura repulsed then pulled me in, and I closed the gap between us. My steps were mired down by the molasses stickiness permeating the air.

Step, slide until I reached the snake charmer. *Step, slide* until I reached the one who had achieved statuesque in the middle of summer.

"Are you okay?" I asked.

Such a simple question, yet the words caused black slitted eyes to notice my intrusion. Hollowed out fangs menaced with deadly promise. Serpentine syllables flicked their way through thick air, each hiss trying to cling to the hem of my shorts. I thrashed the attackers, pushing past my knees quickly and with precision, but it was no use.

It was then that unfocused pupils expanded with surprise. The girl's attention snapped to my fluttering hands, which were still unconsciously removing the invisible threat.

"It doesn't help. Nothing helps. Better to let them take what they want," her voice, lifeless as her eyes.

Ancient strength constricted with an audible slither. No longer were the girl and the beasts in tandem. Domination was the entity's new objective, and a human would not win. When she spoke up, her fate was sealed.

Traumatic brain injury is a long phrase, at least long compared to the thud marking its arrival. Seven syllables take a few moments to form, time enough to watch a person's skull crack against the pavement.

Trau-mat-ic brain in-ju-ry = thud

Her blood loss wasn't affected by the humidity. A steady scarlet stream blossomed underneath her body. The porous cement embraced the red liquid. Cradled it. Her skull yielded to the rock that was now its final resting place.

Heads don't bounce but they are somewhat malleable.

As I processed the reality of her crumpled form, skinny trails wound themselves between the girl's body and mine, fleeing from her departing heat. They were me now, and I no longer existed.

The girl's advice would be taken. My new masters demanded much and expected compliance. My temperature adjusted itself, rising ever so slightly, creating the perfect environment for a cold-blooded killer.

Gemini (may 21 - June 21)

An invitation to
a very special
event will come
today   xoxo

Seemingly astute
individuals choose to
embrace ignorance.

It should bewilder,
yet it does not. Without
fail, the lure beckons,

calls to those who would
cast aside thought in favor
of total blindness.

∞∞∞

Decomposition
of the fraying thread that holds
your life together.

The Flock that Tends

It started on a Tuesday. I know my recollection is accurate because Gram made pancakes. She concocts those lopsided circles every Tuesday, and every week I refuse to eat them. Something about consuming a food that fails miserably at being round makes me gag. The bumps and lumps and uneven texture . . . disgusting. Just thinking about her pancakes raises my gorge.

Regardless of the inedible fare served that day, something odd happened. My neighbor ran off.

Ms. Dawsey rarely left her house. I knew because I kept an eye on her front door. Each time she emerged, cotton skirts swirling around stick-thin ankles, I rushed over to claim my prize. And that prize came in the form of a cookie. Chocolate chip, sugar, peanut butter—all were possible options. Where my grandmother failed at preparing a perfect circle, Ms. Dawsey did not.

I'm not quite sure of the magic she conjured during her baking endeavors. I only knew that each of Ms. Dawsey's cookies tasted as divine as it was symmetrical. If only the secret of roundness could be shared with Gram.

That strange Tuesday, the peculiar Tuesday that started it all, my lovely neighbor exited her home in an unusual rush. I ran across our adjoining lawn and called out as she was climbing into her car. "Ms. Dawsey! Ms. Dawsey, wait!"

She paused, looking bothered. "Oh, Simon. I didn't see you. What do you need dear? I'm in a bit of a hurry and need to head out."

"A prize, Ms. Dawsey. I came over to get one." *How was it not obvious to her?*

She shook her head, frowning. "My sweet boy, I'm sorry. I haven't had time to bake. I know how you like your cookies just so, which takes a lot of patience. But things have been keeping me busy lately. I'm afraid there's no prize today."

I couldn't think of a single thing to say. Couldn't fathom the wrongness of the situation. Couldn't articulate the perplexity bouncing around the corridors of my mind.

My silence was interpreted as a cue to leave. Ms. Dawsey smiled in a distracted way as she closed her car door, and pulled down her driveway, heading toward a town with hundreds of destinations. There were numerous places where my befuddled neighbor could turn up, and I wasn't sure which one was correct.

The most logical answer was to investigate. Rationality was the conqueror of perplexity. It wouldn't do to have this issue unresolved.

Being careful not to dirty my jeans, I removed a rusty key from a dying potted plant on my neighbor's back porch. Slight resistance met me as I unlocked the door and clambered over the threshold. My entrance sounds echoed up and down a meticulously clean hallway.

Despite the lustrous floors and the dust-free surfaces, a rancid odor assaulted my nose as I stepped further inside. The scent led me to a closed door, behind which I knew was Ms. Dawsey's bedroom.

While I had been invited inside on numerous occasions, the bedrooms were never an area of exploration. The dining room was where we spent the majority of time, eating sweets and sipping on chocolate milk. To trespass beyond that realm of familiarity sent waves of trepidation down my spine. But I continued on. For Ms. Dawsey.

I pushed open the door and uncovered the source of the smell. Dirty plates littered the bed and dresser. Curdled milk filled neglected glasses. Sheets of paper crinkled under my shoes.

Judging by my neighbor's distractedness and the state of her bedroom, I guessed something was amiss. The reasoning behind this something was unknown at the moment, but Tuesdays were unfilled by appointments, and there was ample time to investigate. *I sure could use a cookie right now.*

In addition to the paper cluttering the floor, several pieces were taped to the walls. Most were computer paper with rows of typing, but a few were clipped newspaper sections. As I approached the rectangles of text, the contents became visible.

> *Gemini (May 21-June 21)*
> *Saturday: Today will be a*
> *day of self-realization. Open*
> *your eyes to the possibility*
> *of a new relationship, which*
> *may come in an unexpected*
> *form. Embrace the unknown*
> *and harness your energy*
> *into a productive manner.*

> *Gemini (May 21-June 21)*
> *Wednesday: A recent*
> *development will continue*
> *to blossom. Seek wisdom*
> *from newfound sources and*
> *open your eyes to the*
> *possibility of greatness.*

Horoscopes. This contrasted sharply with the neatly pressed, apron-wearing matron I knew. Maybe she sought some sort of excitement in her life. Prior to this moment, I thought she found stimulation in the mystical properties of proportional confections. Undoubtedly, I was wrong. It seemed my dearest neighbor sought inspiration in the stars.

I turned my attention to the typed pages hanging on the wall. As I read the first, and the second, and the twentieth letter, a pattern emerged. Ms. Dawsey had been exchanging messages with an individual named Bert for a period of months.

> *My dearest Bert,*
>
> *I lovingly count the hours since I stumbled upon your musings. How they have pointed me in the right direction. I used to spend my days tending house and baking, but now life has more meaning. You've seen to that.*
>
> *The day we meet, will be the day my purpose has been realized.*
>
> *Fondly,*
> *Camille*

All of the letters spoke of a higher purpose. All of the letters spoke of the day Ms. Dawsey would meet this Bert.

This information wasn't particularly alarming by itself. Although my neighbor was elderly, I knew that even she needed companionship beyond that of a teenage boy. But taken together with her odd behavior and untidy room, these communications hinted at something far more nefarious than a burgeoning friendship.

Bert's replies were not displayed on the bedroom walls. Judging by the level of devotion evidenced in her words, I knew Ms. Dawsey hadn't thrown them out. They must be tucked away somewhere.

Her food-covered nightstand contained a bundle of paper held together with a yellow ribbon. I untied the bow and removed the first letter.

> *CAMILLE,*
>
> *THE DAY GROWS CLOSE. TOGETHER WE WILL MEET OUR DESTINY. CONTINUE TO READ THE PROPECY AND I WILL CONTINUE TO SPEAK THE WORD.*
>
> *REGARDS,*
> *BERT*

What an intriguing letter. I hadn't expected the mention of destiny and a prophecy. And Bert's attention was slightly different than Ms. Dawsey's. His letter appeared to be a bit more . . . selfish. No, that's not right. His words were mission oriented. He had something to accomplish. The rest of his notes contained the same types of messages.

I had to find out more about this person. Had to investigate deeper. Had to figure out if Bert was a dangerous sort. My neighbor depended on it.

With the letters tucked into my pocket, I locked Ms. Dawsey's back door and sprinted a block north. Every week, my grandmother and several other ladies met at Mrs. Updike's home for cards and coffee. They fancied themselves a gang of grandmas and referred to their gathering as the "Gaggle of Gorgeous Gals". Too much alliteration for me, but if it made them feel nice, I could ignore the obvious bad taste.

My knocks were answered with haste. "Simon! Is everything okay? You were banging so hard on the door, I thought it was going to break," Mrs. Updike panted.

"I need to come in. I need to come in *now*!" I flung my arms in the air, hoping to show her my seriousness.

"My heavens, I've never seen you act like this before." She raises her painted on eyebrows and takes a step back. "Should I call Maude?"

"No! Please, Mrs. Updike. It's important. And I don't think I have a lot of time. My grandmother won't be able to help."

"All right. Come in. Tell me what's so important."

In a room full of doilies and decorative plates and stuffed cows, I brought Mrs. Updike up to date on my recent discoveries. She let me unleash the information without interruption, all the while nodding in the right places. When I was finished, she finally spoke.

"Do you feel better, son? Talking it through has always helped me. I have some pecan pie and vanilla ice cream in the kitchen. Would you like some?"

"What? *No!*" I stopped, remembering my manners. "I mean, no thank you. I just want to make sure Ms. Dawsey is okay."

"Dearie, Ms. Dawsey is in love. Now, I'm not 100% sure that Bert is the right type of fellow for her, but she sure is taken by him. It's all she talks about during our gaggles." Mrs. Updike pauses to think. "Well, she hasn't made it to the last few, because she's in such a tizzy with him. But when she was coming, it was 'Bert this' and 'Bert that'. I liked hearing it. Made me feel young again." She fanned her reddened cheeks with a hand.

A slammed my fist on the couch arm. "But she never forgets to give me a prize! And her bedroom was filthy! Do you have any idea where I can find Bert? Maybe if I talk to him everything will make sense."

"He works at the newspaper. Writes obituaries and sports and horoscopes, I think." A grin lights up her face.

"Since you're in such a tizzy, I bet can find him at work on a Tuesday afternoon."

I ran for the door without saying a goodbye or thank you, exiting Mrs. Updike's home with a new direction. The newspaper office was a mile away which would give me time to think of a plan. The horoscopes on the wall now made more sense—Ms. Dawsey had been following Bert's writings in the paper! I was still unsure of what the prophecy was, but if I was going to find out, Bert the reporter would be the person to ask.

I couldn't just burst in on someone. Even my frazzled brain knew that. I needed to convince Bert I was a friend. An individual he could confide in. Maybe I could go undercover like MacGyver? He always solved the case when me and Gram watched reruns on Wednesdays.

The walk to the press allowed my heartbeat to slow to a normal pace. My breaths no longer came in gasps and my brain fog dissipated as I formulated a plan. I forced myself to smile as I walked through heavy glass doors, pretending I wasn't nervous. Pretending I was there on a mission.

A receptionist kindly pointed me in the direction of the nearest restroom. I washed my hands three times for luck and looked sternly at my reflection in the mirror. *Ms. Dawsey is depending on you.*

My hometown is quaint and friendly and has a low crime rate. Or at least that's how it's marketed to potential residents. Those characteristics worked to my benefit, because the newspaper building was compact with only a few offices.

Bert's door bore his name. I knocked primly, professionally.

"Yes, who is it?" A rumbling voice called out.

"Just a fan, looking for Mr. Abrams. I was hoping to speak with him, maybe share some ideas."

The door swung open to a grinning face. The man was tall. And handsome. Exactly the sort of man the ladies on my soap operas fell for. He waved me in. "Come, come. I always have time for my fans. Let's get to know each other." Bert pointed to a chair near his desk.

The first portion of the plan went surprisingly well. No cops burst in on me demanding to see my papers or warrant or whatever they would want to show I belonged. But now, it was time for the complicated part. I had to be tricky. A manipulator. Not my usual straightforward guy.

I swept inside and sat in the closest chair. My legs trembled, but I pushed through. "Mr. Abrams, thank you for letting me barge in without notice. I had to come over as quickly as possible because I noticed a message in your writing. And I wanted to run it by you."

He ambled to his desk, leaning on the edge inside of sitting. "You can call me Bert, son. And what is your name?"

"Um, my name is Chris. Chris Smith," I stammered.

"Well, Chris Smith, tell me what message you think you saw." Bert said, his smile never faltering. "You've definitely piqued my interest."

"It's in the horoscope section, which I've been reading for a while now, but today was finally the day that everything came together." Newfound confidence took hold, steadying my voice. "I'm a Gemini, and the messages seem catered to me. Like I'm meant to follow some guidance or something. That I'm supposed to listen to you."

"Interesting, Chris."

"I hope this doesn't sound crazy. I just admire you so much, and when I felt like you were talking directly to me, I knew I had to come pay you a visit," I said, trying to make eye contact.

"You know what? You're not crazy at all. In fact, I think you're the sanest person I've spoken to in a while." He stood, straightening his spine to his full height. "Would you like to come to my house to continue this conversation? I can help you understand the message. Because there definitely is one."

The problem with acting like a grownup was that you had to make decisions like a grownup. Gram would be worried if she knew I was heading to a stranger's house. Her worry would be compounded if she became aware of the unusual circumstances surrounding this particular stranger.

But it was for Ms. Dawsey. So, it had to be done.

"Mr. Abrams . . . I mean, Bert, I would enjoy that."

"Wonderful. I'm finished here, so we can leave right away. Let's get going, Chris."

Thoughts raced during our walk to the car.

My speech teacher would be so proud. He really believed my story. I'm going to find out what's happening to Ms. Dawsey!

When the doors locked, and the engine started, my thoughts began again. This time in a different direction.

This is all wrong! That went way too easily. He suspects something.

Zero conversation occurred during our drive. We exchanged no words as we pulled into Bert's driveway. Silence marked our steps, as we crossed the palatial threshold.

Ms. Dawsey stood at the foot of the staircase, wearing a dress that covered her from neck to foot. Her stillness was unsettling, her movements reverent as she took Bert's coat. After an adoring gaze that didn't quite reach her eyes, she departed on soundless soles.

Bert's perpetual grin folded into a malicious smile. "Simon, I knew you might show up eventually. Camille told me she had a neighbor who was unnecessarily nosy. And now, your curiosity has gotten the better of you."

I stayed silent like my surroundings.

"Ah, nothing to say. Well, it seems as though you read the notes I wrote to your neighbor, that simpering cow. Thus far, she's been the easiest to convince of my power. All I have to do is push a little mumbo jumbo out to the loneliest birds in their daily horoscope and they eat it up like stale bread."

He took a step toward me and winked. "I watch the birds, Simon. I watch the birds all day long. And it's gotten me to the place I am today. Look around you." He rotates and lifts his arms at the extravagance around him. "I have fifteen fowl tending to my every whim because they think I'll take them to the promise land. The fucking promise land!"

I noticed movement out of the corner of my eye. Ms. Dawsey stood ramrod straight, glaring at Bert from a shadowy corner. Her adoration had been replaced with raw malice. Her breathing came out in short, ragged gasps.

"It's amazing how stupid some can be, Simon." Bert sneered, his gaze still locked on me. "Yourself included. You know I'll have to dispose of you. Or should I say, my flock will have to dispose of you. Can't have you tarnishing my reputation with fantastical tales, now, can I?"

He turned to Ms. Dawsey, as if expecting her to fawn over his words, but the scream that burst from her throat shattered the artificial serenity. Her face, usually kind and soft, twisted into a mask I didn't recognize as she shrieked in rage. My cookie-making neighbor transformed into a monster, and a small flare of panic rose inside me.

She raised the hem of her dress and sprinted toward Bert, stopping inches away from his confused face. Her sleeves fluttered like wings as she lifted her arms, and the light caught on the knife she was clenching. Her usually gentle voice rumbled out in a roar. "No! No! No! Nooooooo!" Each syllable that emerged from Ms. Dawsey was punctuated by a stab with a serrated kitchen knife. Stab. Stab. Stab.

As Bert's life pooled on the terrazzo tile, her screams died with each stab. Her protests drained from her until the only sound life was metal on flesh. The blood blazed a crimson trail my way, reaching for my feet with each inch it grew.

As sirens began to sound in the distance, I looked down at my newly red shoes. *Now Gram would know I had visited a stranger's house.*

I asked. You answered.
But the words made little sense.
Something about your

slack-jawed expression
pushed my buttons, and not in
a good manner. My

fists clenched, along with
teeth that had previously
been locked into a

smile. Forced niceties
exhaled, but the internal
conflict raged white hot.

∞∞∞

Glass panes allow light
to shine on the horrific
thoughts under your grin.

Buon Appetito

Every time Tommy walks through the Door to Maza-Rae, it feels like a gut punch. Air yanks out of his lungs so quickly, that his body's automatic breathing response startles into a pause. Once he steps over the threshold, the suffocating feeling subsides, and his normal inhale-exhale activities resume. It takes a few seconds at best.

He got used to the sensation over the years, and to be honest, he's come to enjoy the momentary loss of respiratory control. It means that good things are coming. Meaningful things.

His trips to Maza-Rae are always short. He spends five minutes behind the Door once a day. The length of his visits isn't the important part though. It's what Tommy brings back that makes his daily excursions worthwhile.

He strides down a well-worn dirt path, toward a clearing ringed with wispy trees. At its center sits a small pond, the surface glowing with a hint of pink. Almost the color of a healthy intestine. Tommy crouches and rests on his haunches near the edge of the water. As always, each of his hands hold a canteen, his grip around them tight and sure.

He plunges both canisters under the pond's surface, watching the ripples of water caress his wrists. A soft *glug, glug* noise emits from the vessels as they fill, the only sound disrupting his surroundings. When the canteens are topped off, he returns to the Door connected to his other, much noisier world.

When he reaches the floating, dark wooden door, Tommy braces himself for the stomach clenching feeling. He turns the smooth handle and pushes back through the dimensions, pulling tight on the wood to close it tight. Cold air envelops him as he walks through the industrial-sized refrigerator. Goose bumps break out on his arms as he strolls past rows of beef and cheese, but they fade when he enters the kitchen. Humid air smacks him in the face.

Clanging sounds tell him it's close to opening time. Hearty smells tell the same story. He breathes the aroma in, loving the pungent scent as always. Homemade pasta, meatballs, and sauce. It doesn't get any better than that.

A low-pitched voice behind him catches his attention. "Hey, Tommy, did you grab any garlic from the walk-in? We're running low out here, and I need some for the sauce."

Tommy turns to see his new prep-chef, apron stained with marinara and cheeks flushed red. He smiles the man's way, holding up the bulbs as proof. "I sure did, Marco. We can't serve pasta, if there's no garlic in the sauce. I'll bring it up in a few."

As soon as Marco rounds the corner toward the fry pit, Tommy double checks the lock on the walk-in cooler. Snug and tight, just how it should be. It wouldn't do to have his employees stumble upon the portal. They would never understand. Maza-Rae is only for the chosen few.

Tommy tucks the key into his apron pocket. He hurries to the grill line and throws a handful of garlic into a sizzling saucepan, stirring the bulbs until they soften. Then he waits for the food orders to start pouring in. During the two-hour lunch rush, they serve over three hundred plates of noodles, each coming out looking and tasting like Italian perfection. A patron never eats just one serving at Tommy's Pasta House. Average consumption was three heaping helpings of gut-busting goodness.

Every day, halfway through the lunch rush, Tommy ventures from behind the grill and enters the dining room to talk with his guests. He moves from table to table, conversing with the diners, laughing at their jokes, and asking about their meals. Happiness and delectable smells fill the room each time. His heart swells with pride at what he's built.

Today, as he makes his rounds, something wet splashes against his cheek. Tommy wheels around, catching a young boy tucking a water gun into his waistband. A smirk fills the child's weasel-thin face. The boy seems proud of his aim. He doesn't flinch as his mother scolds him. The smirk stays plastered his mouth.

As Tommy approaches the table, the mother's words come into focus. "Why do you always embarrass me, Liam? We came for a nice lunch, so I could spend some time with you, and you had to ruin it by being rude. You need to tell that man you're sorry. Right now." she shakes a finger at him, and her mousy hair bounces.

The boy's expression shifts. Instead of smug, he looks annoyed. His arms cross over his chest, and he rolls his piggy eyes. His mother's words mean nothing to him. His expression makes it apparent.

Tommy glides to their table, smile straining against his cheeks. His interest has been piqued. The day just got interesting. "Good afternoon, ma'am. My name is Tommy, and I'm the owner." He hods out a hand and she limply shakes it. "I'm thrilled that you and your charming boy picked my restaurant as your lunch destination. Is there anything that you need? I'm here to make your afternoon unforgettable."

Her cheeks flush pink, as she opens her mouth to speak. "Thank you, sir We happy to—"

A squeaky voice cuts her off. "Mister, my mom wants me to apologize for shooting you. So, I'm sorry. It was a good shot though." He looks over to his mother, then back to Tommy, and finally down at his tablet. He presses play on a paused video of *World's Greatest Fails.* The restaurant disappears for him as he drowns in the pain of other idiots.

Tommy clears his throat. "You know what I'm going to do? Well, your son's apology touched me so much, that I want to do something for him." He flourishes his hands, catching the boy's attention for a second. Long enough to see his scowl. Tommy continues, putting a show on for the mother with his beaming grin. "I'll personally make his lunch today. He's earned it." With a grateful look from the mother, he takes the boy's order and retreats back to the kitchen.

Speaking with patrons and giving a friendly face to the restaurant was one of Tommy's goals when he roamed the dining room. But his primary mission was more predatory. Every day, he hunts for one special individual, and today that person would be the water-gun wielding brat.

Tommy pours the two canteens of water from Maza-Rae into a pot, bringing it to a boil. Rigatoni is next, and the noodles cook flawlessly in the aqueous blend. Marinara sauce and a sprig of parsley perfect the plate.

Boiling the water from behind the Door awakens the larvae inside. These parasites consume the internal organs of the person lucky enough to ingest them. Slowly, imperceptibly. After years of endless gnawing, the invaders eventually take over all body functions. The original host becomes a shell.

Subtlety was the reason for Maza-Rae's success. When hosts like Tommy change one human a day, nobody notices. Force is not necessary for the takeover, because hosts consume the tiny invaders willingly enough. Restaurants were the perfect front for this species takeover.

Excitement pushes Tommy's pulse up a notch. The boy has no idea what's in store for him. He grabs a tray and places the boy's meal on it. As Tommy approaches the child's table, he looks up from his screen with hungry eyes.

With a flourish of his hand, and a bow, Tommy gently lays the plate in front of his next victim. "Buon appetito, young man. Enjoy."

Tommy didn't have to look back to know that the boy was already shoveling mouthfuls of Rigatoni into his face. And that he would continue to cram his maw full until the plate was empty and the brat's gut was swimming with new life.

What they said about this restaurant was true. People could never get enough of the pasta.

Always shocking to
discover you're not quite as
lovely as you thought.

∞∞∞

Wear the white dress, he
said. The one that lies about
your lost innocence.

I Did Something Bad Last Halloween

I did something naughty last year, but I didn't get caught. And I liked it. Really, really liked it. So, I think I'm going to do it again.

Mommy and Daddy only paid attention to me when they were angry, so I learned to disappear. I got good at blending in with the walls, until I became more ghost than little girl. Children were for seeing not hearing, but I made sure I wasn't seen *or* heard. My disappearing act worked most of the time. I'd go weeks without speaking a single word. But some days my camouflage didn't work and I caught the eye of one of my parents.

On the extra bad days, both mommy and daddy saw me. I hated those days.

My mother took out her anger with her voice. Her red face hardened into a cruel mask before she started screaming. "Caroline, how many times do I have to tell you I want this floor clean enough to eat from? I see spots all over the damn place. You're an even bigger moron than I thought if you think this looks good enough. Get back in here and do it again."

"I'm…I'm sorry, mommy," I stammered, standing tall because I wasn't allowed to slouch.

She sneered. "God, you're so fucking pathetic. Stop with the crying. And don't get any snot on your uniform. You wouldn't want your classmates knowing that you're a blubbering idiot." And she'd storm away into her room, slamming the door behind her.

I know she didn't really want me to clean the floor again. It was already spotless. Plus, the bus would be pulling up to the front of my house soon and she wouldn't want me to miss it. She wanted me to go to school. The hours I spent in class were her quiet time, the time she didn't have to deal with her stupid daughter. Or so she mentioned on numerous occasions.

When she yelled at me about the floor or the dishes or my room it wasn't really about my cleaning abilities. No, her motives were meaner than that. My mom wanted to remind me of how much better she was than me. How much prettier and smarter and talented.

What Mommy didn't know was that every time she pointed her words in my direction, my heart grew just a little blacker. I may have cried in front of her, but my tears had stopped being about pain a long time ago. Now they were about the hot fury building inside me.

My father expressed his anger in a more physical manner.

Both he and my mother were drinkers. Every day they downed a case of beer, cracking the first one at the breakfast table. They didn't chase their pancakes with orange juice or coffee. For them, alcohol was the complement to every meal.

Neither one of them worked, since my mother happened to be the heiress of a sizable fortune from her tragically murdered father. Even alcoholism couldn't put a dent in their inheritance, although they tried their hardest to make that happen. All their money did was supply their booze and hide their cruelty. To everyone but me, they were generous socialites.

The days when the beer was finished before Daddy passed out were the worst days. He'd send my wobbly mother to the store in search of the whiskey he liked, leaving the two of us alone together. Just me and my daddy.

When I heard him slurring my name, calling out to me across the house, I knew to brace myself. But as much as I tried to be strong, to be tough, to not care, I always ended up crying when my father was done with me. He liked the belt best, but his fists were often his backup weapon. He never hit where the bruises could show. He was caring enough to do that at least, although it was more for his benefit than mine.

But last year I had figured out a way to feel better. No more anger. No more emptiness. No more pain. Only justice.

A story my mother had told me when I was nine years old inspired me. It was Halloween night, and I was allowed to go trick or treating with some neighborhood children and their families. I hadn't trick-or-treated last Halloween because of my parent's drunken stupor, so I was excited to roam the streets with grownups who were nothing like my mother and father.

My bag of candy started to get heavy as the night got later. Every house we stopped at seemed to give out the most magical treats. And everyone was smiling and laughing. The evening was so different from my ordinary existence.

When my friends and I started to slow, the adults knew it was time to turn in. As much fun as I was having, I knew that I needed to sleep before school the next day. I wouldn't want to oversleep and miss the bus. My mommy wouldn't like that very much. So, I said goodbye to my friends and went home, with my head full of memories and my hands full of candy.

I knew my parents would be drunk and sleeping at the late hour, so I approached the house quietly. When I opened the front door, I heard a loud breath. The kind that you make when you're startled awake.

It was coming from the couch. And as I locked the front door behind me, footsteps approached.

"Why the hell are you coming home so late?" My mother's voice poured over me, stinking of beer. She lumbered over me like an enraged bear.

"I'm sorry, mommy. I didn't have my watch on, and didn't know it was so late," I tried to appease her. Sometimes it worked.

"That's no excuse! Get your ass to bed, now." She pointed toward my room with a sharp finger.

I started to move away from her, hoping those words were all she had in store for me. I must have turned too quickly, because the sack holding my treats swung from my shoulder and crashed onto the floor. Dozens of pieces of candy spilled out, covering the carpet and my mother's shoes. Terror froze me. I waited for my punishment, barely breathing.

"Caroline. Turn around and look at me." Her voice was ice cold.

I forced my body to obey the command, although everything inside me wanted to run away. When I found her gaze, her face was contorted in rage, and her eyes were darting back and forth between me to the candy.

"What is your problem?" she asked, narrowing her eyes. "You come waltzing in and have the audacity to throw this trash on the floor right in front of me? Pick up your mess this instant! You will learn to respect me."

Shuddering, I dutifully picked up each piece, treasuring the memories I had created while gathering the red, blue, and yellow wrappers. I wouldn't allow them to be overshadowed by this witch.

After I finished, I looked up expectantly at my mother. I knew there would be more.

"Caroline, you know what they say about Halloween candy? How dangerous it is?"

I shook my head.

"Yes. It's incredibly dangerous. Every year, certain children are given candy that has something wrong with it. Some pieces have razors inside. Others have deadly poison mixed in with the chocolate. No matter what's been done to doctor the candy, the children that eat the special pieces die. Their insides get cut up or they vomit from the cyanide and wither away." She leans closer, her hair greasy dangling close to my body. "The children selected are the ones that deserve it. They're the rotten little brats, the ones everyone secretly hates."

She stopped talking for a moment, her lips slowly pulling into her heartless grin. "I bet there's a special piece in your bag. There has to be one, because you're the worst child I've ever met in my life." A cruel laugh cuts through the air. "Guess what? You're going to eat each and every single piece of this candy, right now. And you're not going to bed until we see if you live. Or die. You know which one I'm hoping for."

I did what my mother demanded. I didn't die, but I ate every single piece of my candy. I ate so much that I threw up over and over, begging my mother to let me stop. She was true to her word though. She forced me to continue until I'd swallowed every last bite.

It took me a few years, but I finally learned a valuable lesson from that story. The special candy! The special candy was for the worst children. The ones who pulled my hair or called me names or who didn't know what it was like to grow up with parents who only wanted to hurt you.

I knew plenty of kids like that. They were in my school and on my block. It would be easy to select a few.

The first batch of my tampered candy came out lumpy and misshapen, and it was impossible to put back in the wrappers. I needed a new plan to get it right.

I used the library computer to look up recipes for chocolate bars, and I bought the ingredients with money I stole from my dozing mother's purse. Two ingredients I didn't need to buy were already at my home—razors and arsenic. The first for Daddy's daily shaves, the second for the mice in our basement.

I laced all of the chocolate with poison and placed small, jagged pieces of the sharp metal in my concoctions. Using the wrappers from the failed first round, I gently placed my special treats inside and sealed them just right.

On Halloween night, I was allowed to go trick or treating on my own for the first time. I skipped about, darting from group to group, slipping pieces of chocolate into open bags as often as I could. I made a dozen pieces, and I passed them all out.

The first was to Jamie, who lived two houses down. Her mother always welcomed her from school with homemade snacks and a smile. It wasn't fair that my own mommy only greeted me with insults.

Hope you like chocolate, Jamie.

The next piece was for Sean. He once held me in the coat closet, pushing his sweaty hands into my stomach, pressing his slimy lips onto mine. What right did he have to touch me? None.

Maybe this candy will help with your awful breath, Sean.

After that, I lost track of where the pieces went. It didn't really matter. All of the children I picked probably had a better life than mine. An unfairness that made me boil with rage. That Halloween night was when they were going to hurt just like me. They would become my brothers and sister through pain.

I arrived home in a whirl of anxiety and excitement. What if I was caught? And what's worse, what if my candy didn't work?

But it did. Oh, it did.

Reports of hospitalizations started rolling in less than an hour after I finished trick or treating. Children who had eaten their special candy before bed were brought to the hospital for emergency surgery.

Most lived, but one unfortunate did die. It was Sean. Sean who thought he could treat me how he wanted. Who thought my mouth was his to claim.

He was wrong. His life was mine to claim.

∞∞∞∞

This Halloween, I need to be careful. Although it's been almost a year since Sean's death and the multiple hospitalizations, parents are still wary. As the holiday grows closer, news stories have been circulated and flyers passed out, reminding the entire town of what transpired. I kept one of the flyers. Folded it and placed it in my underwear drawer where no one would find it.

My parents gave me permission to go out of town for Halloween this year. One of my childhood friends had moved away, and I made a big show to Mommy and Daddy about how much I missed them. I think they finally relented not out of empathy, but out of a desire for a child free house. They were happier when I wasn't around.

My thirteenth birthday is a few days after Halloween. I know as the years trickle on, I will look less innocent. No one suspected that a child was behind the deadly horror last year. Every person the police questioned resembled those washed-out men you see on wanted posters,

The creepy old men who looked like they would follow your children in a van, offering puppies to lure them in.

But me, with my blonde curls, blue eyes and sprite-like height, well, I was inconspicuous as pie. I guess that's one thing I can thank my parents for. They taught me how to blend in, and I used that lesson to my advantage. I've also learned that a sweet face can disguise even the darkest of hearts. And mine grows darker every day.

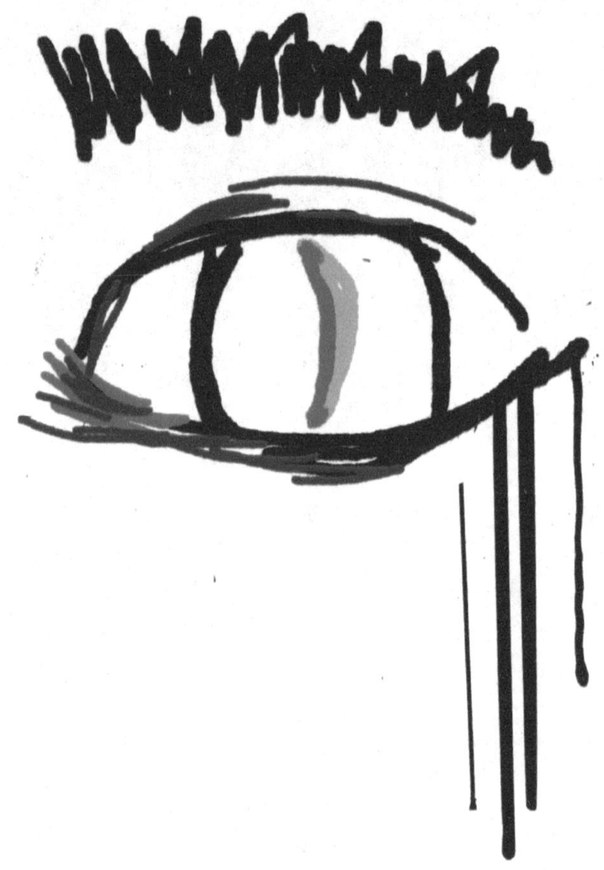

It's possible to
run with the speed of neglect
and forgetfulness.

∞∞∞∞

The poison of deep
self-loathing is slow to build,
but devastating.

Once the lure has claimed
a victim, escape becomes
ineffectual.

Its grasp soils any
normalcy. Its demands burn
through entire lives.

Embrace the shadows,
and dark eroticism
will corrode your heart.

The path is thinning,
saturated with peril;
no reprieve in sight.

A labyrinth of thought—
twists, turns, dead ends. To emerge
is to truly learn.

Forgiving oneself
requires persistence, but
freedom tastes divine.

He Had Sharp Eyes

I loved quiet relaxation after a busy day. It was meditative and revived my energy. After leaving work and picking up the kids, I often rewarded myself with stillness and calm, just for a few minutes. Sitting on the couch, snuggling under a warm, woolen blanket does a fantastic job of melting away the frantic stress of the day.

While I relaxed, my children were one of two places. In their respective rooms entertaining themselves or outside in our backyard. Our rental had several windows facing the backyard, which eliminated any unease. I could watch them while I unwound, see them run around the oaks or swing to the clouds on their swing set.

They were both still young enough for their imaginations to be on fire and I enjoyed hearing about their adventures during dinner. I'd be refreshed from my quiet time, and they'd be elated from their backyard play time. It made our evening meal quite pleasant.

After one particularly trying day, the couch felt extra comfortable. The gentle woosh of my breathing lulled me toward the land of sleep. I've dozed off before and I learned to have the foresight to set an alarm for twenty minutes out.

It wouldn't be a smart idea to sleep through dinner or the nightly bath and bedtime ritual. I heard Tanya and John outside, gleeful and happy, so I let my eyes close and I drifted off into darkness.

My alarm sounded and I woke feeling wonderful. It's amazing what twenty minutes of shuteye can do. It was a Friday night and since my nap invigorated me, I thought it would be fun to grab pizza at the kids' favorite restaurant. It wasn't often I could afford that luxury, but I had worked a few hours of overtime last week and I was feeling spendy. I couldn't wait to tell the kids.

Quiet greeted me when I opened the backdoor. Every other time I had ventured into Makebelieve-ville laughter or voices welcomed me. But today there was a heavy silence in the air.

I noticed Tonya's shoulder peeking out from behind an oak tree, so I called out to her. "Sweetheart why don't you and your brother come inside and wash up. We're going for pizza tonight."

Twenty seconds passed without a response. The silence swallowed my enthusiasm, turning it into dread. *Why wasn't my girl moving? Why was she just standing there?*

Fear quickened my steps. I reached Tonya in a few seconds and turned her toward me. Her eyes were blank. She stared at a spot over my head, high off into the clouds. She wouldn't or couldn't look at me. "Tonya? Darling? Are you okay?" I gently shook her shoulder.

Widened eyes snapped to my face, her trance changing into rigid panic. "Oh, Mommy. It's you." She pointed toward the swing set. "John is gone."

Fear ripped through my heart. I hadn't noticed John's absence until she spoke. Her needs were my only focus. But now the void was obvious. Her brother wasn't where she pointed, or anywhere else I could see in the yard. "Where did John go? Are you two playing hide and seek?" I asked hopefully.

She swallowed hard. "He came and took him," the words whispered out.

I grabbed her shoulders, forcing her to look at me. "Who came?"

"The man," her whisper barely made it to my ears.

My welling tears spilled onto my cheeks, trailing down until the fell into the dirt. Someone came into my yard and abducted my son. My sweet boy, the one who never complained. And I had been sleeping while it happened. Sleeping and leaving my children vulnerable to some man.

Tonya leaned toward me, her pupils shrunk to pinpricks. "His eyes were sharp, mommy."

"Sharp?" Thoughts raced through my mind, none that were pleasant or comforting. "Did he have a weapon?"

She shook her head. "Just his eyes. If I woulda kept looking, they would have cut me. Just like they cut John." She stopped and guilt disfigured her face. "Mommy." Her voice trembled along with her body. "I had to look away. I didn't want the man to hurt me. But when I stopped being scared, and looked back, John was gone." Sobs shook her body, her tears joining mine in the dirt. "I'm sorry, Mommy. I shouldn't have looked away. It's my fault."

I grabbed her and held her close as we hustled inside. I had to call the police, but my girl needed comfort. I could at least give her this. "No baby, it was mommy who looked away, not you. Nothing is your fault."

She flashed a hollow grin, then sat on the couch with a blank stare, humming the theme song to her and her brother's favorite cartoon. With trembling fingers and a cracked voice, I called the people who I hoped would get my son back.

***

The police searched for days but nothing turned up. There was no evidence, no trace of the man who had stolen a piece of my heart. They eventually moved their resources to other cases. More solvable ones.

I got Tonya into therapy as quickly as I could. She stopped blaming herself as time went on. Her nightmare grew further apart until they happened once a year at the most.

As for me, I knew that my daughter was right about the man. Every night, I saw his eyes in my dreams. And they're sharp all right. Sharp enough to cut.

Joy costs less than pain.

The two can intermingle,

but if you dig, dig,

dig to pain's heart,

you'll discover the rotten

root, the driver of

many who lash out

at joy, because it exists

and they can't find it.

∞∞∞∞

Each day, her sunshine
kisses push me toward good. I
cannot fail her trust.

The Electrician's Dilemma

Darcy Gray stared into a cup of lukewarm coffee, sinking into his chair. The light hanging above his head flickered a steady beat, and long shadows filled the space with each pulse. The dimness in the room matched his mood. Somber, tired, irritated.

The lights were dim for a reason. Since last week, his sector had been operating at half power, each house given enough watts to "function" but not enough to actually function. His manager at Lecton Light harped on the deficit every day, and Darcy knew this morning would be no different. He hated the daily lectures, and he usually built up the motivation to work another shift during breakfast, growing his resilience with each sip of coffee. But today, he listened to another type of lecture, this one delivered by his wife.

Zoë leaned across the table, boring her eyes into his. "Our budget is tight, darling, but we need a new car. The wagon has already stalled three times this week and once was on the way to get Delia from school." His wife wrinkled her nose, pushing back a strand of auburn hair that had escaped her tight bun. "The room mother gave me an awful look. Only five minutes late, and she acted like I was the world's most neglectful parent."

Darcy raised his eyes to meet his wife's irritated gaze. "From what you tell me, those room mothers are a judgmental bunch. I bet Delia didn't even notice you were late. The adults always get upset about these things, never the children."

Zoë stomped her foot under the table. "Darcy, that's not the point, and you know it." Her voice grated his ears, high pitched and reedy. Her red flowered dress reflected off her pale skin, giving her cheeks a fiery flush. She looked manic. Sounded it too. "Have you checked our bank account lately?" She raised a thin brow.

He nodded, relieved to have the correct answer. "I did last week. Wanted to make sure we're on track for our summer trip. I was happy to see that we'll have everything covered."

"Yes, yes, we have enough for vacation." Zoë waved her hand, dismissing his words. "But Darcy, have you been listening at all? We need a new car, and we don't have the money to buy one. This is a huge problem."

Darcy drew in a deep breath, held it for a moment, then exhaled. A small ache throbbed at his temple. Another migraine? He hoped not. The last one sent him to bed for the day. There was no time for rest if he needed to make money.

He smiled at his wife, not giving in yet, but softening. "What should we do, dear?"

She grinned, looking pleased, but her green eyes drilled into Darcy's as she answered. "I asked for extra hours at work and got them. Unfortunately, even with that boost, my paycheck won't make a difference to our bottom line." She reached across the cherrywood table and gripped her husband's hand. She squeezed his knuckles together. "I know you don't want to hear this darling, but I'm going to say it anyways. You must pick up the slack. Our family needs you to step up in a big way."

Darcy was good at his job. He wasn't Lecton Light's highest producer, but he placed in the top quarter every month. The money he earned from his rank kept food on the table and afforded his family an annual vacation. This simple life was enough for Darcy. Dominance had never been his objective. In fact, he loathed the techniques used by the Apex Eight, the Electricians who reigned supreme at Lecton. He preferred a less destructive approach. Something milder.

Zoë's opinion differed. She constantly pushed her husband to become promotion-minded, wanting him to scale the monthly rankings to the top. The money would be better, she was right about that, but Darcy wasn't one to compromise his morals. It was a sticking point in their marriage, and he knew she was about to bring it up again.

Zoë leaned back in her chair, placing her linen napkin on the table in a pile. She raised her chin and steeled her voice. "I spoke with Kitty yesterday, and she told me about this month's bonus. It's double the normal amount, Darcy. We could easily afford a car with the extra, and then some." Although her next sentence was a question, Zoë fired it off like a command. "What if you put your ideals aside, just this once, and earned some extra points? Kitty showed me the leaderboard, and you can place first if you give it all you've got. Can you be the man I need you to be today?" She squeezed her husband's hand again, eyes glinting with need.

Darcy despised Kitty Conrado and her braggart husband, Paul. Although they lived across the street, Darcy maintained enough distance to escape their drama blackhole, being polite when he needed to, but offering nothing beside pleasantries. At work, Darcy did the same. He wasn't obvious about it, but he avoided Paul at meetings and during assignments. His life was easier without the couple's presence. Quieter. Yet, here the Conrados were, being brought up by his wife during breakfast. So much for avoiding them.

Darcy jaw tightened, and he barely kept the annoyance out of his voice. "Can we leave Kitty out of our discussion? Just this once. Please." He took a breath, forcing oxygen and calm into his lungs. Getting upset would only make things worse. "You know I'm not fond of the Conrados. They're in everybody's business. And if we share our troubles with them, the whole neighborhood will know them in no time."

Zoë pushed her lipstick-stained lips into a pout. "Kitty was only trying to help, darling, and honestly, it wasn't in her best interest, because Paul can win without trying. For us though, Kitty's willing to take the loss. She hates that her favorite neighbors are in a pinch."

His wife shot from her chair and strode to the kitchen counter. She picked up a piece of paper from the tan surface, holding the corner with her fingernails. When she returned to the table, she slapped the sheet in front of Darcy, speaking while he read the information. "As you can see, Paul is poised to win the summer jackpot." Her finger stabbed the braggart's name on the printout.

His wife's voice grew louder as she continued. "But—and this is a big but, Darcy—if you increase your output, you can overtake him. It means making two or three extra stops, but if you score big at each location, you'll rocket up the ladder." Zoë wagged a finger at Darcy, and he was reminded of his mother's constant scolding. He was never good enough for her either. "I know you like to make smaller plays, and yes, that gives us enough to get by. But now isn't the time for restraint. We need a reliable car, darling." She raised her eyebrows and lowered her voice. "What if the station wagon fails while Delia is in it?"

Darcy winced at her words. Delia was six, and she meant everything to her father. Placing her in harm's way wasn't an option, Zoë was right about that. "Okay, you win." He bowed his head, ignoring the throbbing in his temple. "I'll earn as many points as I can today. I'll talk to some of the other Electricians and see if they have any tips for upping my score too. They're ruthless, but maybe they'll share some pointers."

Zoë squealed, sending a jab to his skull. "I knew I could count on you. Thank you for taking care of your girls." She leaned down to plant a kiss on the top of his head before grabbing his half-filled mug. She returned to the kitchen, whistling as she strolled.

"Thank you for breakfast." Darcy rose from his chair, needing an escape. "I'll go wake the sleepy head."

He tiptoed to his daughter's room, a purple-walled space decorated with outdated maps from Second Earth. Darcy gathered them at work when assignments brought him near antique stores. People in the mirror dimension loved collecting old items, a practice he didn't understand until gifting Delia her first map. Her eyes had lit up like it was Yulemas. Her smile had been glorious. The twelve maps he'd given her since then were tacked to the wall, framing her white, canopied bed with a geographic flourish.

Delia loved seeing remnants from a world that matched her own. Most weekends, Darcy and his daughter used the maps to plan trips to towns with names like Waterproof and Bitter End, places called T64 and C790 in their realm. They traced roads and mountain ranges, laughing at the silly differences between Second Earth and their home.

Darcy glanced at the relics before bringing his eyes on his daughter's sleeping form. He listened to the measured whoosh of her breathing, beaming at her wild hair and twisted sheets. She slept how she lived—with all her might. For a moment, Darcy observed the rise and fall of her back, allowing the ache in his head to fade. Then he knelt by her bed and sang, "Wakey, wakey, little girl. It's time for you to rule the world."

Delia popped up, alert in seconds. "Daddy!"

"Hey, sugar plum. You ready for breakfast and school?"

"Do I have to go to school?" she asked with a titled head and sparkling eyes.

"Yep. You sure do." He tapped her forehead with a gentle finger. "You've got a big brain, and you're going to do good things with your smarts." He rose, holding out a hand. "But first, you have to finish kindergarten

She threw back the covers. "Okay, Daddy." She stood and grabbed Darcy's fingers, her warm brown skin matching his own. "We're building forts today, so that will be fun."

"That sounds like a lot of fun." He guided her to the dining room, where breakfast waited on her favorite purple plate. "I'll see you later, Delia. When I get home, you can tell me about your fort." Darcy placed a kiss on her forehead, breathing in her sweet scent. "I love you."

She grinned and blinked hard, scrunching her nose as she closed her eyes. "Love you too, Daddy." Her focus changed with the speed of youth. Her eyes shifted from her dad to her food. She devoured a mouthful of scrambled eggs, switching to grapes for the next bite. After she swallowed, she sipped her juice, bebopping her head the whole time.

"You eat like your dad, sugar plum. I like finding my food's rhythm too." A chuckle rumbled from Darcy's throat as he turned to his wife. "I'll do my best today, Zoë."

She laid a hand on his chest. "I know you will." She touched his cheek with barely-there lips, and whispered in his ear, "Good luck. I'll be rooting for you."

Darcy gave a curt nod, and Zoë and Delia waved while he hurried out the door. He snapped a mental picture of the perfect moment, his girls smiling and sending him off. Warmth filled his heart as he walked down his driveway and slipped inside their failing station wagon. If all went well today, he'd earn enough to buy a replacement vehicle. A safer one. No one in his family would have to drive the faulty wagon again.

Thankfully, the car started on the first attempt, and he shifted into gear without issue. After pulling onto the freeway, Darcy switched his brain into autopilot, something he did often on the route he had driven for over a decade. He needed to formulate a plan during his commute, so he kept the radio off and thought through his options as the miles passed in silence. None of the alternatives were appealing. If he wanted to make more money, he would have to cause real damage during his shift. Getting close to the Apex Eight's level meant erasing hope for his targets, and not just a smidge, but a whole lifetime's worth.

He tried to calm himself, breathing deeply as the miles flash past his windows. A single day of callousness, that's all it was. Darcy knew he could do it. Physically do it, at least. He worried about the aftermath, about how long his actions would haunt him. A sick feeling roiled his stomach. He needed resilience to handle what he'd put in motion, and he wasn't sure if he possessed enough strength to overcome what had to be done.

◌◌◌◌◌◌

Sixty workers, all dressed in coveralls and boots, gathered in the basement for roll call. The group was diverse in gender, age, and race, but these factors didn't matter at Lecton Light. Rank formed the only hierarchy. The dream of attaining Apex status motivated most Electricians. Of course, some employees were content with their position on the bottom rung. Management called these folks the pyramid base, a critical team who supported the higher-ranked producers.

The guys in Apex Eight called them chum, and they looked down on the lowest fifteen, reserving their most scathing commentary for this group. Plebes were what they called the remaining Electricians. When they were in a good mood, that was. When they were angry, ranks nine through sixty were deemed shitbags, scabs, or LPs, the last insult an undefined mystery.

While it was possible to rise through the rank structure, the Electricians at Lecton Light existed in an almost homeostatic environment. The same people had comprised the Apex Eight and the lowest quarter since Darcy could recall. Some movement happened in the middle ranks, but even there, Electricians shifted up or down a single digit, never jumping more than two spots at a time.

Darcy, number Fourteen, socialized close to his rank, gravitating toward Electricians Thirteen, Fifteen, and Seventeen during his work hours and even in his off time. Today, however, he scanned the room, searching for Nine and Ten, men outside his social orbit. Men who fancied themselves closer to Apex than their fellow plebes. Men with ambition.

Darcy spotted them sitting together, heads bent over an item laying between them on the plastic break room table. Their hair was a similar shade, so they resembled a brown blob welded together by the scalp. Whatever they were studying had captivated their attention. They were immune to the bustling around them.

Darcy shuffled over, holding his breath until he drummed up the courage to greet them. Forced cheer colored his voice. "Hello, Rylan. Tom. Good morning."

The men ignored him, keeping their eyes fixed on the object in front of them, what Darcy could see was a book. *This was for Delia's sake*—he reminded himself before trying again, this time adding an appeal to their humanity and a boost to their egos. "Sorry to bother you guys, but could you spare a minute for a down-on-his-luck-dad? It would be an honor talking to you both, because either one of you can break into Apex whenever you want. That must feel awesome."

Tom flicked his eyes up. "What's your name, old man?"

Darcy gritted his teeth. He had worked with the duo for five years, and they weren't much younger than him. Still, they possessed the knowledge he wanted. Playing by their rules was necessary. He kept his tone pleasant when he answered, nudging aside the annoyance he felt. "Darcy Gray. I'm number fourteen." He stuck out a sweaty hand but let it drop after the offering went unacknowledged.

"We know your rank, plebe." Rylan yawned, leaning onto the table with an elbow. "But we don't waste bandwidth on your personal details."

"Got it," Darcy replied, cheeks warming in humiliation. He glanced at his other coworkers, but no one had noticed their conversation. They were all scrambling to eat breakfast or slurp down coffee before the day began.

"What do you want?" Tom waved the book in his face. "As you can see, we're busy."

Darcy read the title—*The Impact of ACEs*—and wondered what the men were studying. He pushed past his curiosity. "Do you have any advice for improving my strategy? The wife needs a new car, which means I need massive points today." He nodded at the pair. "You're

Electricians I admire. You're both creative and have tons of knowledge to share."

Tom smirked. "What makes you think we'd share anything with you?"

"Yeah, Fourteen, you're a slacker. We notice stuff like that." Rylan crossed his arms over his chest. "You're a dude who puts in the required effort, nothing more, nothing less. There's no way you could operate at our level."

Darcy ignored the insult and pleaded one last time. "Please. I need to score big for my daughter. The new car is for her. Well, for her safety." Determination filled his eyes as a new steadiness filled his voice. "You think I'm a slacker here, but at home, I give everything to my family. They want for nothing."

"That's the motivation you need to bring here, old man. No sense hoarding it at home." Rylan's too-red lips twisted into a smile. "How 'bout we help him, Tom?" He nudged his friend's right arm, the one holding the book. "Let him read how to get ahead at Lecton."

"Great idea." Tom slid the text across the table where it stopped in front of Darcy. "Read some of this. Three let us borrow it last week, and we're already making gains."

Rylan glanced at his watch. "There's ten minutes before roll call. Happy reading, Fourteen."

Darcy accepted the offered book and made his way to a quiet corner, leaning against the wall. He didn't trust Tom and Rylan, but there was little choice this close to go-time. Over the past few days, the duo *had* edged closer to Apex. Just yesterday, Tom missed eighth rank by three points, the closest an outsider had been to the top tier.

Maybe the book held their secret. Maybe they were telling the truth.

With hope blooming in his chest, Darcy raised the navy and gold tome close to his face. The book was heavy, like the yellowed encyclopedias he saw when buying Delia's maps in Second Earth. He read the title once more before opening the volume: The Impact of ACEs.

What in the world were ACEs?

The first page defined the term—adverse childhood experiences—and it highlighted how terrible they were for a person, causing issues for a lifetime. There were several ACEs, and as Darcy read what they are, unease crept through his body

Child abuse. Neglect. Drug use by a parent. Violence. Parental imprisonment. All the worst things that could happen to a child. Everything he kept his daughter away from.

What were Nine and Ten doing with this information?

Darcy's gaze flicked from the book, locating the Electricians. They must have been waiting for his reaction because their mouths opened in a laugh, and their eyes—Rylan's green and Tom's sharklike, almost black—locked onto his, taunting him. The pair knew he would find the book repulsive. Their laughter showed how little they cared for him. They would probably spread the story of his sensitivity to the others by the day's end. Another joke on him.

But Darcy couldn't let that bother him. It was past time for compassion or caring. His only focus was on gaining points and earning that bonus. He must push aside his feelings for his little girl. She needed safety, and damned if he was going to let two wannabe Apex losers drive him from this goal.

He slammed the book closed and advanced toward Nine and Ten. Their smiles melted from their faces as they watched his approach. Their eyes narrowed, losing the haughtiness from before. Now they were watchful. The slight tilt of Rylan's head said curious too.

When Darcy got close enough, he tossed The Impact of ACEs into the air. Both men scrambled for it, limbs flying in movements that would be funny in other circumstanced.

Tom snagged the text before it hit the ground. "Why'd you do that, Fourteen? That book is valuable." Tom flipped through the pages, ensuring everything is intact. "We were just helping you out, man, since you sounded so desperate about your wittle girl."

"Yeah, you came to us boo-hooing, and all we did was give you something that can make you a better Electrician. It's not our problem you couldn't handle it." Rylan crossed his arms over his chest and stood taller, trying to look more impressive than his average build. "That's the last time we help you, Fourteen."

"Good. I don't need your help if it means I have to hurt people." Darcy matched Rylan's posture, stretching to his full height, something he rarely did. The world wasn't built for the very tall, and 6'7" Darcy usually slouched to adapt. But sometimes his extra inches were a benefit. Like today. Rylan and Tom leaned away from him, not backing down, but putting space between them.

Undeterred, Darcy closed the distance, lowering his voice in volume, but not in intensity. "Are you abusing children? Please tell me you're not causing them harm like it says in that book."

Tom winced. "What? No. You know the rules." He pointed to the front of the room. "We don't break them. We just bend them a little."

Darcy snapped his eyes to where Tom was pointing. A ten-foot frame dominated the wall, the document inside the frame filled with words in a black, capitalized font. These were the Electrician's Rules. There were five. Lights trained on the document made them impossible to ignore. It was the first thing employees saw when they entered the break room.

Like the other Electricians, Darcy had memorized the rules, but he read them silently while he contemplated his response to Tom.

1. ELECTRCIANS WILL NOT CAUSE DIRECT HARM.

2. ELECTRICIANS WILL BLEND INTO THEIR SURROUNDINGS.

3. IF CONFRONTED, ELECTRICIANS WILL USE WHATEVER MEANS NECESSARY TO RETURN TO THEIR HOME DIMENSION.

4. ELECTRICIANS WILL ONLY USE PORTALS TO CLOCK IN AND OUT OF THEIR SHIFT.

5. TARGETS ARE TARGETS; POINTS ARE POINTS; YOUR LOYALTY IS TO LECTON LIGHT.

Based on the book Nine and Ten loaned Darcy, adverse childhood experiences counted as direct harm. If a person abused or neglected a child, that was without a doubt hurting them. There was no bending the rules here—they were clearly being broken if Rylan and Tom were using ACEs to grow their score.

He swung his head toward the men, advancing another step. They shrunk back in response, and a small thrill blossomed inside Darcy. They were afraid of him. Good. "Is that how you two are raking in the points? By trashing rule one and causing chaos in Second Earth?" Darcy asked.

A caramel-smooth voice interrupted his questioning. "You've got it wrong, Fourteen." Darcy turned his head to the left and Blythe Robbins filled his vision. Number Three's raven hair was piled high on her head in tight braids. Her hands were planted on her hips, and she held her chin high. The challenge was clear. "No one is hurting anyone. We're just facilitating a path toward desperation." She rolled her almond-shaped eyes. "I've never even touched a Second Earther. I don't need to. They make my job easy."

"Then what's up with the ACEs book? Why do you need to know what creates trauma if you're not causing it yourself?" Darcy snapped, not backing down.

"God, you're dense. You literally couldn't be more LP if you tried." Three shook her head. "We don't cause anything, Fourteen. We just nudge Second Earthers in the direction that inflicts the most damage. You know that the more potential a target loses, the more energy we can extract." She lifted her chin higher, sneering at him down her nose. "If we place drugs in front of a recovering addict, is it our fault if they relapse and hit their wife? Or if I keep a parent awake overnight by playing a recording of annoying noises, am I really to blame if they snap and yell at their kid?"

Fury ignited inside Darcy. He clenched his fists to keep from reacting. Punching the other Electricians would feel incredible, but the consequences weren't worth it. He had to stay calm for Delia.

"Of course you're to blame." Darcy glared at his colleagues, trying to decide if they were serious or not. Were they not seeing the implications of their actions? Were they really that dense? Or selfish.

"Riiiight, Fourteen." Three smirked at him, confident in her actions.

Nine and Ten still shrunk back, but their expressions had shifted from wary to haughty. Three's support had given them a confidence boost.

They were a lost cause.

Rage sparked in his eyes as he leaned close to the trio. "You might think that what you're doing isn't hurting people, but you're wrong. Every action you take to 'nudge people' is harming them. But I can see you've made up your minds." Darcy lowered his voice, hissing between his teeth. "I'll be watching you out there. If I see you doing anything like what's in that book," he shoved Tom's hands, knocking the heavy text from his grip, "I will report you."

A ring shrilled out before the argument could progress. The sound cut through the break room, halting conversations mid-sentence. The warning bell. It was briefing time.

Darcy and the other Electricians hurried to the front of the room where the Head Electrician waited. Erik wore a royal blue jumpsuit like everyone else, but the outfit looked commanding on his muscular form. There was no mistaking him for a meter reader. He wasn't a tall man, but he put off a tall aura. He made even the most lumbering giant feel small, Darcy included.

Erik's steel gray eyes sharpened his presence. No one wanted to be on the receiving end of one of his stares. Bad things happened when he fixed you with his gaze. Reprimands. Firings. Rumor even spoke of a beating, where he'd left an uncooperative Electrician bleeding on the break room floor.

The Head Electrician's voice cracked through the group. "It's the last day of the month, and I expect results. Sector six is down to half power, and we need at least

400,000 watts to put a dent in the deficit." Erik pointed at One, a lanky brunette with a permanent sneer. "All of you need to be more like this man. He eats potential for breakfast, lunch, and dinner. Do you think he cares about our targets? No. He only cares about serving his people." He swept his arm around the room. "Our people."

Head bobbed around Darcy, and energy simmered in the air. The speech captivated the group, even the slackers who barely skated by. Their boss knew what he was doing. He knew how to motivate.

"Now, I'm not telling you to break the rules. We don't touch our marks or cause *direct* harm." Erik winked at the word direct, aiming the wink at Three, Nine, and Ten. Darcy peered at the trio in time to see smug smiles marring their faces. Their arrogance disgusted him.

"What I'm saying is, be creative with your methods. Gluttony, purposelessness, and boredom plague the people on Second Earth. Use this to your advantage. Build them up before draining as much potential as you can. And then…" Erik smashed his hands together and the sound of smacking flesh rang through the room. "Then you squash them like a bug."

Silence met his words until Rylan started to clap. In a moment, everyone joined in, even Darcy, although his clapping was subdued. He was distracted.

Erik's speech ran through Darcy's mind. Not the words, but the feel. The incitement.

The Head Electrician was right.

For just one day, Darcy needed to forget about the Second Earthers. His focus should be on his family. Delia's sweet smile flashed in his mind. She was his purpose, not the people in the mirror dimension. Family came first. He could ask for forgiveness later.

A shout from Erik pulled Darcy back to the break room. "Who are we?"

"Electricians," the room roared.

Erik pumped his fist. "What do we do?"

The answer rocketed through the space. "Collect potential."

The Head Electrician planted his feet on the ground and cupped his hands around his mouth. His words came out in a boom. "Are you ready to work?"

"Yes!" The room vibrated with a sound crescendo. Energy crackled between bodies. Everyone was fired up.

"Get out there and make it happen!" a red-faced Erik shouted. He rotated left, striding toward a neon green sensor on the wall behind him. When he placed his palm against the lock, rectangular compartments began to rise from the floor.

Their Vessels were crafted from bylap, a metal stronger than anything found on Second Earth. The strength was necessary for the Electricians' travel between the dimensions. Years ago, weaker materials had caused physical impairments during early test runs. It turned out interdimensional travel was molten hot, and bylap prevented the inferno from seeping in. The journey also bent the mind, and the metal helped with this too, stabilizing the compartments as passengers ripped through the veil.

Electricians lined up behind the ten Vessels, six in each row. Darcy was usually in the back, but today he shoved himself behind Rylan, becoming second in line. The lanky man looked over his shoulder and glared at Darcy. "I'd say good luck, but I know you won't need it. You don't have what it takes to win."

"Watch me." Darcy pressed his elbow between Ten's shoulder blades, and the man winced as Darcy pushed to the front of the line. He whispered loud enough for only Rylan to hear. "You might be surprised with what I'm capable of."

His Vessel's door whooshed open, blocking Rylan's reply. Darcy strutted forward, resisting the urge to glance over his shoulder at Ten. Instead, he quickly locked his feet to the floor with the waiting belts, and typed his destination into the blinking computer screen: 34.6° SW, 0.25° E. Last time he'd visited this location, he'd been alarmed by the number of people slumped on the streets. Pain and distress emanated from almost everyone he came across. He'd walked until he found a hopeful neighborhood, but today he didn't need hopeful. He needed to visit humanity at its lowest.

After he placed his arms in the safety rings and gave them a tug, the door slid shut behind him. As the Vessel hummed, a familiar bristling sensation rippled up and down his limbs. His arm hair stood on end and his toes curled inside his black boots. A minute or so passed, and his heart settled into the double beat that meant he was approaching the breakthrough point. The compartment moved so smoothly, that the *boom-boom, boom-boom* pulsing through his veins was the only indication that something remarkable was happening.

When the vibration under his feet stopped, he knew he had arrived. Electricians are only dim while their heart does double time, so Darcy raced to unstrap himself before he lost his transparency. As he pushed the exit button and emerged from the Vessel, he saw his worry was unfounded. Even if he were in his solid state, there was no one around to view his abrupt arrival. The streets were empty.

Except they weren't quite empty. There *were* people around him. One slouched against a stop sign in a stupor. Another curled up on a bench, a newspaper pulled over their head to block the glaring sun.

Then again, maybe empty was right, as in devoid of emotion. He couldn't make up his mind. These people were certainly missing the zest that made them human. They were sad souls existing and not living.

He looked at his feet and peered at the glittering sand marking his entry point. The ordinary dirt held a wonderful secret, and he liked the contrast. Sometimes the doorways to Second Earth were scenic. They existed inside caves or behind waterfalls, and Darcy became mesmerized by the beauty as he crossed the threshold into the mirror world. Once, he entered through a door in the center of a wildflower field. The spot brimmed with asters and daisies, whites, blues, and yellow crowded together in a living bouquet. That entry point had been cold, the temperature not matching the surrounding area, like something in the air knew about the marvel hiding among the blooms.

And here, where Darcy needed to return when today's shift was over, here was a waypoint that held no scenery whatsoever. He stood in a spot where the road never came clean. People could sweep it or hose it down, but the sand would always cling to the portal. Darcy didn't know the science behind the doorways, he just knew that the portals existed, and that they were glimmers into an amazingness above his comprehension.

After his Vessel retreated to the breakroom for its next passenger, Darcy reached down to tap his belt. When his fingers hit the cool metal cube in the center—bylap again—he grinned. His retrieval pod was ready. So was he. Confidence surged through his body. Today he would dominate.

Cell by cell, the solidness returned to his body. He stepped away from the portal, heading toward the center of the block. Putrid whiffs rose from the garbage lining the streets. Discarded food, plastic bags, needles, and clothes. He avoided the heaps piled on top of the sidewalk, sticking to the street instead.

"What are you doing here?" a voice croaked behind him.

Darcy whirled around and almost fell into the trash he was trying to avoid. The man who had been slumped against the stop sign was now less than two feet away. He recognized the long, greasy hair that flowed onto the man's dirt-stained sweatshirt.

For the second time that day, Darcy rose to his full height, and stated Lecton Light's standard reply. "Hello there. I'm here on a call. I came to fix the lights a few streets over." He offered the swaying man a smile, trying to calm the situation, not wanting to flee like Rule 3 demanded in an out-of-control encounter.

"No." The stranger swung his head back and forth, tangled strands flying around and smacking against his cheeks. His eyes burned with mistrust. "No, that's not…that's not right. You came from air," he slurred out.

"Sir, I'm just trying to do my job. I mean you no harm." Darcy's voice was steady, but his stomach was tight. A Second Earther had never confronted him before. Sure, people passed by from time to time, but they were usually satisfied with a smile and a wave. Darcy was trustworthy because he wore a uniform. He looked like he belonged, and passersby never questioned his purpose.

But the stranger in front of him wasn't fooled by his official looking coveralls or his official sounding words. He must have seen Darcy's arrival through a drug-induced haze, and in a rush of bad luck, the stranger decided to pursue. Darcy needed to convince the man of his legitimacy, to reassure him that everything was fine and dandy.

Or there was another option. He could start earning points.

The third rule said confronted Electricians must return to their home dimension immediately, but what if the confronter was no longer a threat?

Darcy smiled again at the man. "What do you mean, sir?" He quickly scanned the streets while the stranger responded, hoping for an obvious answer to his dilemma.

"You came from air. I…I saw it. I saw everything." He gabbed handfuls of hair and pulled, jerking his head back and forth between his shoulders. "I'm gonna tell. I'm gonna tell them all." He wobbled a step backward, but Darcy reached out and caught his elbow.

He wanted to yell at the man, to shake him and drop him into the street to die alone. To push him through the jagged glass of the nearest house. To drag him behind a boarded-up store and kick him until there was nothing left to kick. Rage flowed through his veins, heating him up and driving him forward.

But Darcy couldn't do it.

As much as he wanted to win, to see his daughter's smile, and know that she was safe in a new car, he just couldn't do it. Instead of hitting the stranger, he brought the man to his chest, wrapping his arms around the shaking body and squeezing gently. He didn't want to steal this man's potential. He wanted to boost it. Maybe it would get him out of being reported or maybe it wouldn't change a damn thing. Either way, Darcy was done draining a world that was already in so much pain.

His words were soft. "Listen, sir. I know life hasn't been kind, but I think there's a spark of good left inside you." The stranger's breath hitched against Darcy's chest.

"Yes, that's right. You are good. You aren't done telling your life's story yet, I know it."

He releases the stranger, and steps back. "I'm Darcy. What's your name?"

"Art." A tear trails down his cheek, cleaning away the dirt in its path. "My name's Art." He lowers his head and kicks the ground. "I haven't been hugged in a long time."

"Well, you deserve that hug and more. You deserve another chance, and just from talking to you for this short time, I know you have it in you. You have the potential." And it was true, because Darcy hadn't robbed the man of his possibility.

"Thank you." Art's words have less of a slur, and he'd become steadier on his feet. "Thank you for seeing me."

Darcy squints his eyes. *Was the color coming back to the other man's cheeks?* When Art first confronted him, pallid skin hung loosely from his jowls. But now, a healthy pink color tinted his cheeks. He looked healthier. And happier.

A vibration came from Darcy's middle. The retrieval pod hummed to life against his waist. He glanced down and saw the pod's gauge rising, flying past 100 watts, to 1,000 in a blink, far past anything he'd ever harvested. *Was his machine malfunctioning?* He needed to get alone so he could investigate.

"Art, I hate to leave you, but I have to head to that job I was talking about," Darcy says, shrugging his shoulders. "It was nice talking to you though. Your future is bright, that's a guarantee."

"A job. Right." Art laughs and winks at Darcy. "Don't worry, your secret is safe with me." He shakes his head and runs a hand through his bouncy hair. "I won't waste whatever it is you passed onto me. That's a promise." He smiled while he raised his arms above his head, stretching far, releasing the tension from his time in purgatory. "I haven't felt this good since before I started using, and that was probably six, seven years ago. You're the man, Darcy. Thank you, friend."

"Good luck, Art." Darcy waved, then pivoted toward a rust-colored two-story house. He picked up his speed until he was jogging then sprinting, flying past discarded filth. His pulse ratcheted up until it sang in his ears.

When he reached the sagging home, he followed a toppled chain link fence through the weed-filled backyard. Brambles snagged his pants as he moved to the concrete pad that must have been a patio in better times. Alone and in the shade, he unfastened his belt and brought the retrieval pod close to his face, expecting the worst. But the machine blinked green from a light at the bottom right corner. Green meant all systems go, which meant nothing was wrong with his pod.

Confused thoughts hurtled through his mind. He double-checked his reading, verified that it showed 1,000 watts, and his thoughts raced even more. *How was he extracting a level ten times higher than normal?* All he did was hug a man instead of harming him. There was no converting lost potential into electricity like he'd been doing for the last decade. In fact, Darcy did the opposite. He increased the potential inside Art. He watched the down-on-his-luck addict turn into a smiling friend in the blink of an eye.

It was like magic.

It was like energy.

The realization smacked him in the face. The happiness, the warmth, the new possibilities—it all provided more excitement for his targets. Which was now the wrong word; client was better. But when his clients experienced more excitement, the retrieval box did some reverse science, and bam! He was not only fueling up his pod, but he was also fueling the people he ran into.

His hands shook as he fastened his belt across his midsection. For the past decade, he had actively spread hurt. Yes, he chose to complete his work on a moderate level, never pushing into Apex Eight territory. But still, he hurt people he didn't need to hurt. His new discovery showed him that there was a different way to power his home planet. A more humane way. There was no reason to spread pain. He knew that now. And he was going to spend the rest of his shift atoning for his past. No longer would Darcy Gray be a drain on humanity. He was now going to elevate as many people as he possibly could.

For the next hours, Darcy hugged and prayed and played, whatever his clients needed. The gauge on his belt shot from 1,000 to 5,000 to 23,000. The gauge on his heart grew even more. He was so used to witnessing sorrow, that the laughs, smiles, and dancing his clients showed him, brought him to tears. Happy tears, of course.

Usually, after a shift, Darcy trudged, but at 6:00 PM, he almost floated back to the entry point. His heart started the familiar double beat as his ride approached. The glow of helping others filled him from head to toe. He was beaming, joyous about his experience.

Until he stepped into the Vessel and realized he would have to tell the other Electricians what happened. Many of them would match Darcy's enthusiasm for a better way of collecting electricity, but there were others—the Apex Eight, Rylan, and Tom to name a few—who would be less than thrilled about his discovery. They were the ones who reveled in the harm they caused, greeting each day with a pain-inspired sneer. This group would fight him. They would push back on what was right.

Maybe Zoë would have some advice. She would be thrilled about his score, and in her happiness, perhaps she would tell him how to reveal his revelation to the higher ups at Lecton Light. She was much better at talking to people than he was. Darcy got tongue tied, and he wouldn't want to do that during such an important breakthrough.

Yes, that was the way. He would tell the Electricians whatever it took when he returned, because he knew there would be questions about his score. Later, at home, he would discuss the issue with his wife and use her advice at work the next day.

Darcy's panic dissipated when he made the decision. He whistled as he buckled his feet in and punched in the breakroom's coordinates. He grinned the entire way back, basking in the knowledge that he didn't have to compromise his morals to win. He wasn't like Nine, Ten, or Three. He was Fourteen, and proud of it.

As the doors hissed open, Darcy heard a rumbling sound from outside. He stepped onto the platform under his Vessel and scanned the room. Every Electrician stood in front of him in a half circle, hands pounding together in a tidal wave of uproarious applause. He quickly found Nine,

Ten, and Three in the crowd. They were clapping, but hardened eyes and pressed lips revealed their true thoughts.

The Head Electrician strode toward Darcy, arm stretched out. Darcy met his palm and shook the offered hand. After a moment, Erik dropped the handshake and raised his arms, waving them to catch everyone's attention. The applause died off, and Erik's voice filled the silence.

"We've witnessed history today, ladies and gentlemen. Your fellow Electrician took what I said about squashing Second Earthers, and he ran with it." He waved Darcy closer. "Take a look at this man. He's nothing special, and for the past decade he's been in the middle of the pack." Erik reached down and grabbed Darcy's arm, raising high. "But now, he's your number One. And if that doesn't motivate you, I don't know what will."

Applause starts in the middle and forms a crescendo before crashing into Darcy. He offers a dazed smile to his colleagues, but he remains quiet. He won't offer anything, unless they ask.

Lucky for him, they don't. After thirty seconds, Erik lowers his arm and fixes Darcy with steely eyes. "Good job, One. Go home and celebrate your ruthlessness. Tomorrow, come prepared to discuss your techniques. We need more men like you out there." He nods before pivoting toward the exit.

When the Head Electrician leaves, everyone else follows suit, clapping Darcy on the back as the head out the door. He expects some disrespect from Nine, Ten, and Three, but the trio departs without saying a word. It was better that way. More peaceful.

Darcy takes his time walking to his car. The twenty-three people he helped today flashed through his mind. Each encounter started with a smile from Darcy and ended with a promise to persevere from his clients. And they meant it. Each person, rejuvenated, hopeful, and appreciative, walked away with a new purpose.

He would happily do that every day for the rest of his life. Work would no longer be something he suffered through. Work would be a lifeline, for him and the people he encountered in Second Earth.

Darcy swung open the wagon's door and flopped into the driver's seat, happily exhausted. The car cranked on the first turn, and he set off for home. He would be with his girls soon.

He pressed the gas as he merged onto the freeway and went back to his cheerful memories as he drove. After a few minutes, the buzzing of his phone brought him back to reality. He pressed answer, and a silky-smooth voice filled the car.

"Enjoying your ride home, Fourteen?"

Darcy recognized the voice. "Why are you calling me Three? Or should I say Four, since I knocked you down a spot?"

"Ouch. For someone who acts so high and mighty, you sure can deliver the insults."

"I give what I get." Darcy turned on his blinker, and merged into the left lane, speeding up to meet the flow of traffic. "I'm busy right now, so make this quick. What do you want?"

"I just wanted to fill you in on a little secret, now that you're part of the Apex Eight." She cooed. "Do you want to know why we called you LPs?"

Curiosity raged through his brain. He wanted to know. Badly. The Apex jerks used LP as an insult, and he'd been called it dozens of times, never knowing what it meant. And now, he was finally going to learn the definition, although it felt strange that Three was willing to share. Just this morning she was being rude to him, but tonight, he was someone she could share a secret with. There must be a catch.

"Why would you tell me? It's not like we're friends," he says, hands gripping the steering wheel.

"No. You're right. We're not friends, and we'll never be friends." She scoffs. "That sounds terrible actually. You're way too old to be a part of our group. I know you cheated today, but that doesn't matter. What matters is that I tell you about our little term of endearment."

"I don't think you were using LP as a term of endearment," Darcy replies.

"Yes, right again. But it's not really an insult like you plebes think it is. It's a label."

Darcy raised his eyebrows. *A label? What did she mean by that?* He tried to take control of the conversation. "Why are you drawing this out? Just get on with it, so I can focus on the road."

She let out a throaty laugh, and Darcy's skin crawled. "Fine. I'll tell you. LP means Lost Potential," she says.

"Why would you call the Electricians that? We're the ones who collect potential, just like you." His pulse raced, and he felt his cheeks redden. Three wasn't making any sense.

"It makes perfect sense, actually." Three lowered her voice almost to a whisper. "Have you ever thought about dimensions, Fourteen? There are much more than two. Much more."

Darcy swallowed hard. His internal alarms were ringing at full volume. He matches Three's volume, barely getting out the words. "I didn't know."

"Well, now you do." A giggle filled the car, and Darcy's breath caught in his throat. Three's voice was high-pitched when she continued. "Let me reintroduce myself, Fourteen. My name is Beatrix, and I'm from dimension two-eighty. I'm an Electrician there too. Of course, at home we call them Seekers. Me and the rest of the Apex fellas came to your dimension because we needed energy, and boy do you losers deliver."

Icy chills ran up Darcy's spine. His vision tried to darken, but he forced himself to focus on the road. If he blacked out, he'd never make it home. And that was all he wanted to do. He didn't need the glory of helping people or the victory of achieving first rank. All he needed right now, was to see his daughter's smile and to tell her everything was going to be all right.

"Why are you telling me this now?" he forced out past trembling lips.

"I'm glad you asked. See, we have different rules on two-eighty. Seekers are allowed to cause direct harm, although most of us prefer the challenge of setting things in motion rather than using brute force." She tsked. "But after today, Fourteen, I realized I needed to do something drastic. We have a pretty sweet gig here, but you messed it up with your meddling, and I can't allow that."

"What does that mean?" Darcy whispered.

"Try tapping your brakes," she drew out the s sound, hissing the word.

Darcy lightly tapped his brake pedal, hoping to feel resistance like usual. But he felt nothing. And still nothing when he pumped the pedal all the way to the floor.

"Now look into your rearview mirror," Three said, almost singing the words.

Darcy pinpointed the white van behind him, the one approaching at a reckless speed. The death-bound vehicle got closer and closer as his eyes stayed glued to the mirror.

A cold certainty filled his body. He would never make it home. His life would spill onto the freeway, and he would become exactly what Three wanted him to be.

He would lose his potential.

He would become an LP.

His car jerked forward as the front bumper of the van pushed into his car. Sparks flew as his car rubbed against the metal median. His last words were gasped into the phone. "Tell Delia I love her. Please."

Her cheerful response drilled into his soul. "Oh, I'll be talking to Delia. But it will be as a Seeker, not as a friend. Bye, Fourteen."

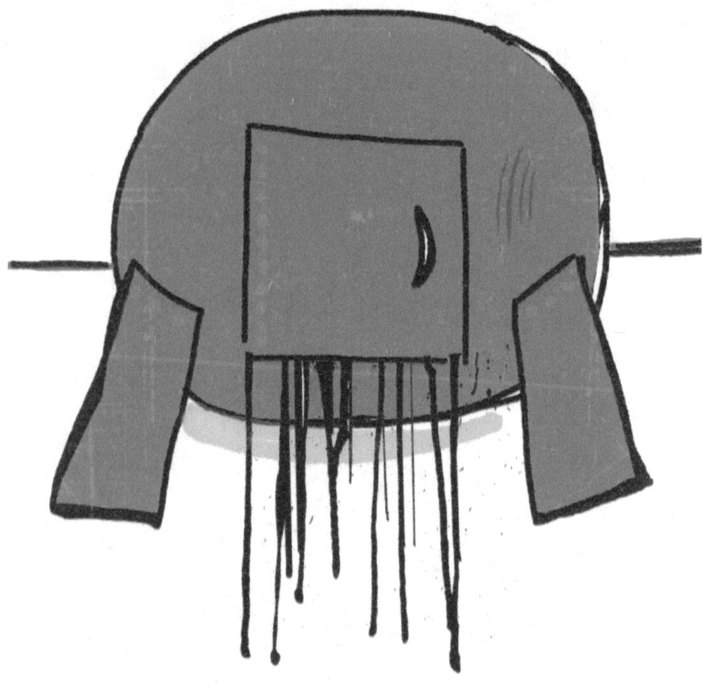

As a puddle forms
beneath feet that gracefully
tiptoe around the

unpleasantries you
left for roadblock purposes,
a shimmer of some

sort of awareness
lights up the gaunt hollows where
approximately

one-third of the drops
hitch before they crash
silently below.

∞∞∞∞

I've hit the edge. The
dark place where niceties fall
wasted between us.

The Chamber

My mother kept weeks of testing and appointments to herself. I didn't know about the poking, prodding, and scraping she endured until a brunch date with a family friend. After pleasantries and mimosa orders, Mom's smile faded, and her lips flattened into a line. She took a deep breath before speaking. "Gary, thanks for meeting us here. I couldn't stand the thought of receiving my diagnosis in your office. I prefer somewhere a bit livelier."

"Diagnosis? What are you talking about?" I asked, swiveling my head between the two. "Someone needs to tell me what's happening."

"Dani, I'm sorry we're springing this on you. Your mother insisted I keep everything a secret until today." Gary shifted his focus to Mom and lowered his voice. "Bethany, I'm afraid it's worse than we anticipated."

Mom laughed, a surprising sound after such a somber sentence. "Nothing stands a chance against this old bird. What's there to be so grim about? Come out with it."

"It's lung cancer." His words were heavy. Blunt. Devastating.

Mom flapped her hand. "Cancer is curable. You know that better than I do." She straightened in her chair, pulling her shoulders back. "I'll do whatever it takes to fight."

"But there's nothing we can do, Bethany." His voice hitched, and he took a moment to collect himself. "If we discovered it earlier, maybe things would be different, but the tumors have spread outside your lungs. Treatment is too risky given the advanced stage." Gary bowed his head. "I'm sorry. I wish I had better news."

Dr. Gary Dashpol had been an oncologist for thirty years. Over the decades, he maintained a stellar reputation and impeccable success rates. He was also a longtime friend of my mother's. I knew that if he said the cancer was inoperable, it was.

I clenched my fists, relishing the feel of nails digging into skin. It grounded me enough to speak. "How long does she have left?" I hated asking such a morbid question but needed the answer. I was desperate to know how much time I had with my mother.

Tears slipped down his cheeks. "Not long. A few months at most. Take good care of her, Dani."

We ordered round after round of mimosas, but the alcohol did nothing to soften the anguish over Mom's cruel fate.

∞∞∞∞

Mom moved into my extra bedroom. While guests once filled the space with laughter, the walls now sagged under the weight of disease. The antiseptic air and hissing respirator kept visitors away. Being reminded of mortality is frightening, and gazing upon my mother's frail body exposed dying's ugly truths.

Mom was proud of her independence, but symptoms emerged within days of settling in. Slowing down became a necessity. The invading tumors stole her essence, turning my mother into an emaciated husk of the vibrant woman she'd once been. Confinement to bed was hard to accept in the beginning, but fentanyl dulled her resistance along with her agony.

After researching my options, I hired a palliative care nurse. Lora kept Mom comfortable and entertained while I was at work. During the first month, crosswords and board games occupied their time. The second month found

Lora reading to my mother during her sporadic bouts of consciousness. Moans of pain and regular doses of narcotics marked month three. Whenever Mom's eyes opened, she would stare at the IV until Lora released the tonic that didn't stop the hurt but at least made it bearable. My mother would sink into a pool of misery without the chemicals keeping her world dull and painless.

Because of her decline, I kept a close watch on my phone during the day. My office was a few miles from home, making emergency response an easy task if it became necessary. Lora knew to contact me if there were any significant changes in Mom's condition, and before today, she'd never reached out.

I was in the middle of an appointment when I felt a vibration coming from my pocket. My patient noticed the disturbance as well. "Dr. Browning, I think someone's calling you. Do you need to answer?" She raised her eyebrows, not attempting to mask her annoyance.

"Nothing's more important than you and your baby, Denise. Let me quiet this, and we can return to the exam." I smiled reassuringly.

The vibrating stopped as I pulled the phone out of my coat. My pulse raced as I noticed Lora's name on the screen, but there was no way I could interrupt the appointment any further. High-risk pregnancies caused anyone anxiety, but Denise was especially apprehensive. Upsetting her might cause harm to both her and her child.

My mother would have to wait. I pressed the power button and tucked the phone away.

"All right. Let's check on your little guy and make sure his vitals look good. We're getting close to delivery, and last-minute surprises are something I like to avoid."

Denise leaned back while I completed her exam. A steady stream of conversation ensured that she didn't notice my increased speed. It also helped distract me and alleviate the panic fluttering in my chest. Every minute I delayed a callback was a minute that could be filled with distress for my mother. Or it could be even worse. Each tick of the clock could be her last.

Luckily the appointment went smoothly, and I discovered no additional complications. I answered my patient's questions about the care her son would need once he was born and ushered her to the receptionist at a pace shy of rushed. "Denise, it was a pleasure seeing you today. I can say with confidence that your baby boy is doing the best he possibly can be doing. Let's chat more next week."

I ducked into the bathroom and turned on my phone. It had been thirty minutes since I'd glimpsed Lora's name, and that time had added two missed calls and three texts to my alerts. Guilt and fear flooded my body. I pressed the call back button and held my breath until Lora picked up the phone.

"Dani! I'm glad you called back. Your mother's agitated and keeps asking for you. You should come quick."

Sharp panic stabbed my heart. "Of course, Lora. Let me take care of a few things, and I'll be right there."

"Good. That's good. Maybe you can calm Ms. Bethany down."

I winced, frustrated that my mother was in pain, and I wasn't there to fix it. "Tell Mom that I love her, and I'll be there soon. Thanks, Lora."

After I cleared my calendar, I sped home, barely noticing the traffic blurring past. I heard muffled noises when I got out of the car, and their volume increased as jogged up the driveway. When I opened the door, an uproar burst from the back corner of the house.

For the past month, my mother spoke in a whisper, but now, her voice boomed through the house. "Daaaannii," she yelled, drawing out my name.

I sprinted to the guest room where Lora was trying to calm my thrashing mother. Her words barely cut through the discord. "She's on her way, Ms. Bethany."

"Daaaannii," she cried, undeterred by her nurse.

"It's going to be okay. I promise." Mom stopped flailing and Lora leaned close, smiling at her patient. "That's it. Now, let's get you settled while we wait. We can't have you toppling off the bed."

I stepped into the room while Lora tucked Mom in. When she noticed me, the nurse's eyes lit up. "Thank goodness you're here, Dani." She placed my mother's hands on top of the blanket, and gave them a gentle pat. "If you don't mind, I need a little break. Your mama had the strength of a twenty-year-old this afternoon, and I am worn out."

"It doesn't have to be a little break. Please, take your time." I moved to Mom's side. "Thanks for taking such good care of her. It means a lot."

"Of course. It's my job to make her comfortable." Lora smoothed the blanket. "If you need anything, I'll be in the living room putting my feet up, but I can always come right back." She glanced at Mom before she left, closing the door on the way out.

I sat on the edge of the bed, unsure of my mother's condition. Her energy was refreshing, but I didn't want to attach expectations to what could be over in a moment. It was better to enjoy her vitality while it lasted. I wrapped my arms around her. "I'm here, Mom."

After a moment, she pushed back, breaking the hug. Her eyes were alert, and they locked into mine. "Cadmium," she whispered.

"What did you say?" I asked, thinking I misheard.

"Cadmium," her voice firm this time. "It's what got me into this mess."

"You lost me, Mom. I'm not sure what you're talking about."

"Dani, I'm sorry. I should have told you sooner, but I've been such a coward." A tear slipped down her gaunt cheek.

Concern flooded my body. "You're the opposite of a coward, Mom. You're the bravest woman I know." I tried to squeeze her hand, but she balled it into a fist.

"Daniela, I don't have much time left. You need to listen to me now." Her harsh tone got my attention.

"Anything you need, Mom. I'm listening."

She leaned back into her pillow, starting out slowly. "Since you were six, you've known that you were adopted. It was nothing I tried to hide from you." I nodded, and she continued. "But what you don't know is your birth story, and that's what I need to talk about. Maybe if I tell you, I'll find some peace before I die."

"If it's not too painful, I'd love to hear about my birth." My pulse sped up. I was excited. I knew so few details about my past.

"Okay." Mom squeezed her eyes shut. When she opened them, tears flowed. And so did her story. "For as long as I can remember, I've wanted to be a psychologist. My ultimate goal was to open my own practice. And that's what eventually happened, but there was one stop along the way that you don't know about." She paused, trying to find the right words.

I wasn't sure what she meant about my birth story and a stop along the way, but everything else Mom was disclosing was old news. My mother was a well-known psychologist, and I'd grown up in her office. In the early years, I would do homework in the waiting room. Later, I worked at the reception desk, gaining job experience for my college applications. Sure, there had been some rough years, where she took too much of her job home or she lost a patient from their own hand, but overall, Mom's practice was a place filled with good memories. I had no idea where this conversation was going.

"Oh, Dani, this is where it gets bad." A fearful look had widened her eyes. "I only hope you can forgive me."

Instead of interrupting her with words, I kissed the top of her head, passing on reassurance with a brush of my lips.

She forced herself to continue. "My internship was at Goldhead State Hospital. I was placed in a unit for women who had been judged criminally insane. These women committed horrendous crimes, mostly causing harm to their children, and it was my job, along with another psychologist, to treat them."

Her laugh startled me. It was so out of place. But when I looked at my mother's expression, I could see that she was bitter rather than jovial. This caustic quality leaked into her words.

"So many of our patients were beyond help. Most days were spent in a triage-like environment, protecting the women from themselves and each other. Violence would break out at the blink of an eye, and not only between patients, but against the nurses and doctors as well. It was a very different place than the calm surroundings I had imagined myself in. I was so naive.

"The 70's were a different time for mental health, especially for the individuals who found themselves in the wards of Goldhead. These people were either hated or forgotten about, so it didn't much matter the types of treatment we were administering. As long as we were keeping the public safe by locking them up, almost nothing was off limits. Shock therapy, strait jackets, lobotomies, food deprivation, isolation - any of those could be used on the patients who gave us the most trouble.

"It was awful in there, Dani. The screams, the smells, the feeling that you weren't making a difference. Some of the nurses took their revulsion and frustration out on the patients. They didn't see them as fellow humans, but rather as animals they were in charge of controlling. You almost couldn't blame them. Women would walk around with feces or blood smeared on their clothes, moaning and wailing. Nurses back then didn't recognize these as symptoms of mental illness, they saw every action as a disgusting habit that was correctable with punishment. And they weren't paid well enough to empathize with the people they were harming or correcting as they saw it."

Mom's voice had grown stronger during the telling, but it dropped to barely a whisper for the next part. "That wasn't the worst thing."

Her story had painted a picture of suffering. I could almost see the asylum as she spoke, emaciated women roaming the halls that had become their home. While the patients were wards of the state, it wasn't the structure around them that prevented them from leaving. Their minds were the prisons, the place they were incapable of escaping. Hearing about the abuse patients had undergone at the hands of their caregivers was horrifying. It was difficult to imagine how it could be worse.

"Tell me, Mom. Don't be afraid." I gently prodded.

"I am afraid, my sweet Dani. So afraid." She swallowed hard. "But it's time to tell you about your birth mother. You have a right to know."

My birth mother? In forty years, I was never given any details about the woman who birthed me. I knew I was adopted, but I was never interested in delving into the origins of my DNA, and my mom never pressured me to learn more. It looked like that was about to change.

Mom's words started slowly, but she gained speed as she spoke. "Her name was Karen Cruz. She was eighteen when she was assigned to Goldhead and she had resided there for five years before I began my internship. Karen started gaining weight shortly after I arrived. Even after only a few months of work, I knew this wasn't a normal occurrence. The majority of our patients were rail-thin from either a refusal to eat or their medications. And I guess from withholding food when it was warranted." The last sentence dripped with guilt. "Karen had started out that way, but she ballooned over the course of months."

I couldn't help interrupting. "She was pregnant, wasn't she?"

"Yes, she was. She was pregnant with you."

Shock resonated through my body. *My mother lived in an asylum? She had been criminally insane?* I needed to know more.

"What was she in the hospital for...Mom?" I didn't plan on the hesitance before I said her name. But it was there. And it was noticed.

"She was pregnant once before, during her last year of high school. Karen hid it from everyone and when it was time for delivery, she quietly had the baby in the woods behind her parent's home. When she came back into the house for dinner, still covered in the fluids of birth, she acted like nothing had happened and sat down at the table ready to eat. Her parents called the police, but by the time they arrived Karen had become withdrawn and wasn't able to answer any questions. The judge declared that she was unfit for trial and she was transported to Goldhead until she could be deemed competent."

The poor woman. And that poor baby. Had the police investigated the incident, or had it been dropped when Karen had been sent away? Had someone harmed her, forced her to be a mother against her will? Or had the trauma of becoming pregnant as a teenager in the 1960s broken her? I had so many questions. The horror of it all must have been showing on my face, because my mother started talking quickly.

"Dani, I was going to take this to the grave with me, but I thought it would be unfair to you."

Rage punctuated my words. "I don't know if that's true at all. Why would you wait so long to tell me? Are you trying to ease your conscience in a last-ditch effort to feel better? That's what I think is going on, because this isn't necessary." I exhaled slowly, attempting to calm the anger that was boiling inside. "Is there anything else you need to say, Mom?"

There was fear in her eyes, but she pushed forward. "When we realized Karen was pregnant, we didn't want her to harm the baby. Looking back, we should have been searching for the father and focusing our efforts on firing him. But we didn't. We isolated Karen and constantly supervised her, to prevent her from hurting another child."

There would be no news of my father in this story. For that I was grateful. A man capable of assaulting a patient was a man I wanted to know nothing about. A planned baby could take a toll on a woman's body. Two unwanted pregnancies must have wreaked havoc on my mother's body and her mind. And there was still more to be heard.

"My superior saw the pregnancy as an opportunity for research. He was always coming up with new ideas that he would employ in our living laboratory. No one ever complained about anything he did, and this was before review boards were taken seriously or there was too much interest by the public. We went along with whatever he said." Her voice hitched. "I should have told him no, but I did as I was ordered."

Mom was beginning to fade. The effort she was expending was a lot for someone who had been almost comatose this morning. I could sense that total exhaustion was near, but I didn't want her to slip away before I heard every bit of what she had to tell me.

"Do you need any water? Or your medicine? I can tell you're not feeling well." I asked.

She shook her head. "No. I can't have my head getting all foggy. I'll make it to the end, don't worry about me." Her eyes closed and she leaned back, but her mouth opened and the rest of the story tumbled out.

"There was a sensory deprivation chamber in the basement of the hospital. Certain patients responded well to short times inside. The chamber wasn't something we used for correcting behavior, it was more a treat for those who had behaved properly. Dr. Carson thought of a new way to use it, though. He wanted to see if restricting stimuli for an extended period had any effect on a newborn.

"For the last month of Karen's pregnancy, Dr. Carson kept her in the tank. He hooked up a catheter, a colostomy bag, and I.V.s to ensure she wouldn't have to leave the room. The days that I worked, I was responsible for changing out the solution she floated in and cleaning her medical equipment. That's what got me sick, Dani. The cadmium we used to treat the tank caused this horrible disease. But of course, I didn't know that then."

She looked to me for sympathy, but when she saw disgust instead, she continued. "To make sure Karen wasn't exposed to any stimulus, I had to place a soundproof box around her head when I was cleaning." Sobs broke through her words. "I hated that box. Hated feeling like I was depriving that woman of everything. She would stand there without moving while I did my duties. Naked and shivering and completely vulnerable. Not once did she try to protest or escape. She had completely resigned herself to what we were doing to her."

The horror of what I was being told stilled my tongue and made any reply impossible. Of course, my birth mother had resigned herself to the torture! What else could she have done? The people she had been sent to, the people who were supposed to improve her mental health, were the ones who were abusing their power. Karen had no one to turn to. She had no one at all.

A raspy voice continued. "The day you were born...well, it was eerie, Dani. Dr. Carson insisted your mother stay in the chamber the whole time. I told him it was dangerous, begged him to let me help, but he was adamant that she remain isolated. Said the experiment would be flawed if we interrupted it now. So, I gave in and waited outside the tank for you to be born.

"After hearing no sounds for hours, we finally lifted the lid to make sure nothing had happened. What we saw was absolute serenity. Karen was sleeping, and you were nuzzled at her breast, content as could be. But as soon as the light touched you, you screeched and recoiled as if you were in pain. Dr. Carson turned off the lights, and you quickly quieted. I thought we would do something to help ease your transition to outside life, but my boss had other plans."

A creaking sound drew my attention to the door. Lora's concerned face peered through a small crack. I had forgotten she was resting in the living room, but it looked as though her break had ended. She noticed my look and pushed the door open.

"Dani, is everything okay in here? It's time for me to leave and pick up my son from baseball practice, but if you need me to stay, I can make other arrangements." She was staring at Mom's tear-streaked cheeks and taking in the mood of the room.

I forced a smile. "We're doing okay, Lora. Go ahead, get your son and have a nice evening with your family."

Lora glanced between Mom and me, nodding her head in understanding. "Seems like you two have some important stuff to talk about. I'll let myself out." She grabbed her purse from the side table and left.

I was glad for the interruption. It had given me a moment to distance myself from the story that sounded like a movie script, but that was actually about my life. This was me being talked about, me who was the daughter of a woman forced to become an experiment, me who had been born in a dark, watery room. My world view had been shattered in the space of an hour, and I wasn't sure if I would ever be able to pick the pieces back up again.

The woman who had allowed this to happen had her eyes closed tight, too ashamed to look at me. She was breathing in short, shallow breaths and clenching her fists. She looked like she wanted to give up. But Bethany had more to say, and I wanted to hear it.

"Finish. I need to know everything." I said flatly.

After a long pause, she obliged. "We kept you in the tank for months. Dr. Carson made a baby-sized box for your head, so the light wasn't an issue again. You were happy in there, Dani. Every time I cleaned, I found you snuggled with your mother, floating without a fuss.

"But you weren't developing right. Babies need to be talked to and have room to move about and explore. If not, they can be delayed, which was what was happening to you. You didn't coo, and of course you couldn't crawl. I brought these concerns up with Dr. Carson, telling him it was time to end the experiment. And although he acknowledged my points, he refused to put a halt to anything, citing the purity of the method he was using. I was tired of that answer and threatened to go public about Karen and her baby, but he just laughed and told me that I wouldn't dare put my career in jeopardy over a criminal and a bastard."

Mom opened her eyes and raised her chin proudly. "That's when I knew I had to take matters into my own hand. Stopping the experiment would be up to me." Her pride deflated quickly though, and her chin sunk almost to her chest. "But it didn't go at all how I planned."

I leaned forward in anticipation, still filled with fury, but also curious to see how it ended.

"The opportunity came during a quiet evening. I knew my boss was out for the night, which meant one less obstacle to worry about. I did rounds and talked to a few of the more coherent clients during the beginning of my shift. Once dinner was served, I made my way to the basement. No one knew what we were doing down there, Dr. Carson had made sure of it. Because she'd been gone for over half a year, Karen had faded from the memories of the nurses. They had stopped asking about her months ago. And no one had known she was pregnant or that there was a new tiny resident below their feet. It was all a big cover-up.

"The release from the chamber had to be done with authority, with the air of someone who was doing what had been ordered of them. I had to pretend that Karen was finished with whatever treatment had been prescribed to her. She would stay in the facility and integrate back into the comings and goings of the hospital. And the baby...and you, would come with me.

"What I didn't foresee was the fight that Karen would put up when I told her we were leaving. When I approached her and the baby, she reached up to grab her box, just like she did during cleaning times. I handed her sunglasses instead and she stared at me blankly until I told her that I was getting her out of there, and that we had to work together to make sure her baby was taken to a safe place. This didn't sit well with her."

My birth mother was being forced to leave a place that she might have considered her home. Her basic needs had been met, and she was able to nurture, or some alternative version of nurture, the child that she had soundlessly brought into the world. The outside had been a scary place, making the lack of stimuli in the chamber a haven of sorts. When her doctor had tried to remove her from the sanctity, lashing out had been her only option.

The sickly voice went on. "Karen screamed. It was the first noise she made since being in the basement, and its volume took me by surprise. I tried to calm her, but she grabbed you tightly to her chest and hunched in a corner shrieking the whole time. And then..." She broke off. "And then the madness started.

"I heard footsteps coming down the basement stairs and a key being turned in the lock. Only one person besides me had a key, so I knew what this meant. When Dr. Carson burst in the room, I expected him to yell at me and demand to know what was going on. But he didn't do that. He stormed right past me and stood in front of Karen.

"He bellowed out his words. 'What are you doing out of your cage? You know you don't deserve to be in the real world. Get back in there like the dog that you are.' He reached for the baby as he was saying these last few words. What happened next has haunted me ever since.

"Karen made a sort of roaring sound and leapt at him. She put her teeth to his throat and ripped the skin away. Dr. Carson was still conscious at this point, and the look of disbelief on his face would have been comical in an ordinary situation, but this was far from ordinary. The look was soon removed, because Karen used her fingernails to detach his eyes from the socket. At that point, he fell to the ground making a man shaped smear in his own blood."

Mom shuddered. "I still see his lifeless form when I close my eyes. And that's not the worst thing. Karen did all of this with you in her arms. She held you lovingly while she ripped a man to shreds. And you didn't make a sound until it was over. After your mother finished killing Dr. Carson, you gave a short cry. That cry was silenced by nursing from a breast that was covered in blood." She whispered. "The blood of your father."

A look of peace washed over Bethany's face and her body sagged with relief. The tears that had been a constant companion during her recounting of the tale stopped flowing as the last words departed her lips. It appeared that confessing had done her well.

But her peace didn't last long. The anger that had been building inside me reached a point where thought ceased to matter. Now, only actions counted.

I lunged at the woman who enabled a monster disguised as a man. The woman who treated my real mother as less than human. The woman who confessed her crimes only to clear her conscience. I lunged and then squeezed until ragged breaths halted and pleading eyes closed. The pulse in her neck went from steady to still. The respirator hissed oxygen to unfillable lungs.

I whistled on my way to the bathroom. Lucky for me, I had a tub that would do just fine. I undressed and lay on the bottom. Scalding water cascaded over my skin, washing away the memories of my deed. I thought about Karen as water sloshed over the sides of the tub, splashing onto the tiled floor. I pictured her floating in the chamber, nuzzling me against her.

Love was her guide to murder. Murder was her way to protect me.

My mind slows as water fills my nose and mouth, until only one thought breaks through my consciousness. *This is for you, Mom. I'm ready to come home.*

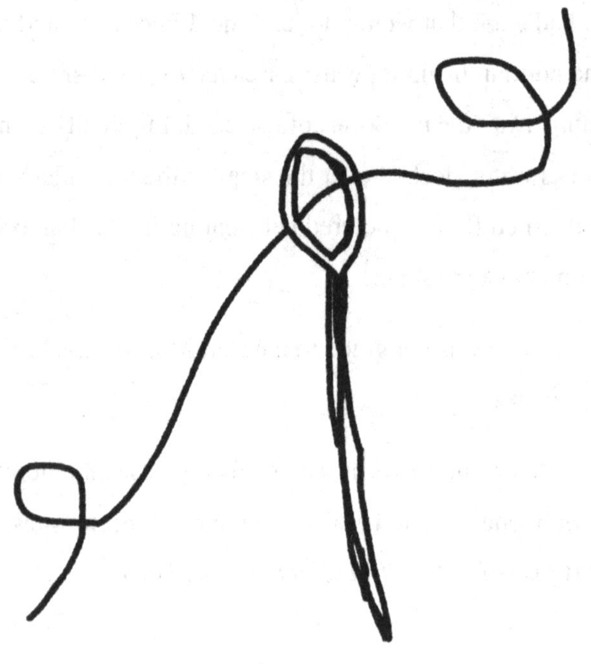

Words lost to darkness.

Uncomfortable history

erased in a blink.

∞∞∞∞

Believe those who tell

you their truths, for they will stomp

on the hard-won paths

your legacy leaves.

Without a thought, they

claim your tale is not worthy.

Silence is your due.

The Fall of Idealia

Once upon a time, in the kingdom of Idealia, lived a merchant, his wife, and their daughter. The Marlock family was prosperous. The father, Dorne, owned a textile business, and his daughter, Arabell, grew up in the storefront. Throughout the day, Dorne talked through every task. He spoke of measuring, smoothing, cutting, and tallying, breaking the instructions into simple terms for the child. The girl absorbed the information and became quite helpful to her father. Her youthful, serious presence delighted clients, and this in turn increased sales.

By the time Arabell was a teen, she handled the store's daily operations. Her father remained in the store, but he napped throughout the day in a nook near the shop's hearth. He woke to greet favorite customers and shout the occasional command, but he left the business's responsibility to his daughter.

Eventually, Arabell became betrothed. Her marriage would take her to a far corner of Idealia, where she would follow her husband to his family estate and use her skills to run a small home-based shop.

On her wedding day, Dorne surprised his daughter with a handwritten book. The tome was bound in leather, its pages gilded with gold leaf. It contained all the merchant knowledge Dorne had passed on, each word recorded in a compact script.

He spoke to his daughter as he handed her the gift. "My child, keep this book close lest it fall into the wrong hands. Treasure this tome, and you shall prosper. Neglect it, and ruin shall fall upon the lands."

Over the course of two days' travel, Arabell moved away from her childhood home. Once settled, it wasn't long before she became known for her goods. Folks in the area flocked to her humble storefront, returning to purchase reams of fabric at a remarkable speed.

Whenever Arabell needed guidance, she opened the book she'd received on her wedding night. Inside, she found answers to any dilemma. Though she did not believe her father's dire warning about ruination, she kept her book close at hand, not wanting to lose the valuable collection of wisdom.

Arabell flourished, but as often happens with prosperity, greed interrupted. Unbeknownst to her, Arabell's every move was tracked by the stable hand, Barlow. From the moment the lady of the house arrived, Barlow believed she was up to no good, and he viewed her success as fraudulent. Over the months, he had observed Arabell reading her book before locking it in a metal box. The stable hand knew Arabell kept the box's key on a chain 'round her neck, and he planned to pilfer it during her next morning ride.

Barlow's plan was executed without a hitch. He waited until his Lady was occupied before sneaking into her room with the stolen key. After unlocking the box and removing the mysterious book, the stable hand fled to his quarters where he opened the tome, giddy with prospects.

The stable hand wasn't the best reader, but he knew his letters and could sound out most words. What he saw in Arabell's book baffled him. The sentences on the first page were written in a language he'd never encountered, and the deeper he went, the stranger the text appeared. Odder still, when Barlow paged to the beginning of the work, the words had altered since his first read. He flipped through the entire tome and found the same was true for each page. A third look through confirmed the illusion.

Barlow was horrified, convinced dark magic was at work. He rushed his mistress's book to the royal palace, where he spoke with the guards about his concerns. After showcasing the tome's powers, the stable hand was given audience with the King.

At first, the King was dismissive. "Stable boy why are you here?" he asked.

Barlow trembled as he responded. "Your majesty, I've brought proof of dark magic. The nastiness has infected my lord's home, and I'm afraid it won't be long before it spreads throughout the kingdom."

"Show me this magic," boomed the King. When Barlow did, the King's reaction was the same as the stable hand's—abject terror at words he could not understand. Immediately, the King ordered the book destroyed.

And so, it was. Arabell's tome was burned, and the ashes thrown down Idealia's deepest well. The King ordered the merchant's daughter to the castle for questioning. When he learned the book had been created by her father, he demanded the cloth maker's presence.

When Dorne arrived in the throne room, he leaned heavily on his cane. The King asked him, "Your book, old man, why did you create such a monstrous item?" Dorne replied, honest as always. "Your majesty, I made the tome for my daughter, to ensure the success of my lineage, long after I die. I've kept a little magic from the days of the fae, and what went into that book was harmless. You could not read the book because it was only legible to those sharing my blood." He drew in a ragged breath. "But now, the magic has been unleashed, and the kingdom shall fall after the full moon rises."

Dorne would say no more when questioned. He was banished to the dungeon with his daughter, and still, he would not speak. Time passed until it was the day of the full moon. Before it rose, Arabell pleaded with her father. "Father, I beg of you, please tell me what will become of Idealia." Dorne smiled, weariness punctuating his words. "My precious daughter, the answer has been here all along. Silence is what will become of Idealia. Just wait and see."

As the moon arced across the sky, words began to disappear from Idealians' throats. No longer could they utter full sentences. Any word that had appeared in the burned tome vanished from the tongue and the mind. The next morning, when cooks tried to follow recipes or teachers attempted to teach, they found the written word incomprehensible. Every text looked to be scrawled in an unknown language, a language that shifted with each read of the page.

"Dark magic!" cried the cooks. "Dark magic!" exclaimed the teachers. Everyone across Idealia marched their books to the castle, where they were denounced and destroyed. As each text disappeared, more words were drained from Idealia, until there was nothing left to say.

Like many kingdoms before it, and like many still to come, Idealia collapsed into itself, and was never heard from again.

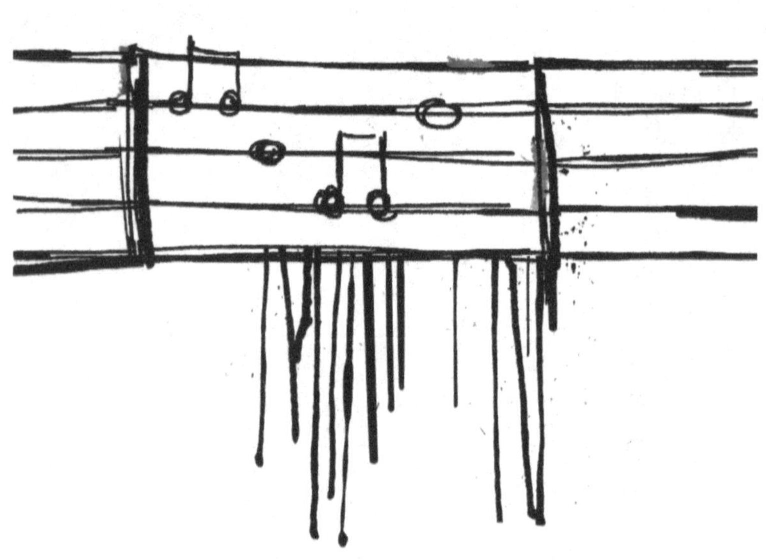

Those most deserving
of love often travel with
only their shadow.

∞∞∞

Close your eyes. Take a
moment to imagine a
never ending wave

of harsh, indulgent,
sex-centric attention that
comes from infinite

directions. So lost
does your refusal become,
you forget your voice.

∞∞∞

Viewed as property,
as a potential good time,
rather than human.

A Smudge

My Sophie was sensitive to the cold. The wheeze of her breathing grew worse whenever a chill tinged the air, and tonight the frosty nip of winter was hard to ignore. It was unfortunate that we had to venture out, but sometimes necessity dictated unwelcome circumstances.

Layers was the answer. A onesie, followed by a shirt and pants, topped with a woolen blanket provided just the right amount of warmth. I gently placed her into the carrier strapped to my chest. Shared body heat brought a rosy tinge to Sophie's cheeks. Downy hair nestled a face round with the fullness of mother's milk. Pink lips rested in a serene smile. She was the image of perfection.

The rhythmic pulse of gentle breathing let me know my girl was resting comfortably. I wrapped a scarf around my face and grabbed the handful of bills I had collected throughout the week. We were ready to leave.

Rather than burdensome, the mile to the store was a joy. Buoyancy marked fulfilled steps and my lighthearted hum filled the frozen air. The gray evening shimmered with shades of promise; never before had dirty snow glistened with such brilliance.

The approving nods of passing strangers affirmed my elation. I had finally gained entrance into the elite club of motherhood, and it seemed as though everyone was supporting my inclusion. Maybe coming outside hadn't been such a bad thing after all. It was a treat to be seen with my girl.

The first weeks of an infant's life were often the most difficult, or so I had read in the dozens of parenting books and articles I had poured over before Sophie's arrival. But the demands of a newborn were tame compared to the countless tears shed over the unfairness of an empty womb. And the pointed questions from others that were aimed at my inability to conceive the child who would make living bearable.

What's wrong with me? I just wanted someone to hold and to love. Maybe those boys were right, Mary Ellen. Maybe you're so ugly that no baby would ever want to come out of you. Fat and stupid. Worthless.

I never did figure out the issue. Sophie's presence had quelled my troubled thoughts. Her every cry occupied my time and left no space for self-pity. For that I was grateful.

A coo startled me out of my reverie. Sapphire eyes, showing a level of alertness uncommon in a one-month-old, gazed up adoringly. Perhaps my negativity had awakened her from her slumber. I would have to learn how to control my emotions. Babies sense these things, another tidbit I'd picked up while reading, and unnecessarily upsetting my daughter was not a very motherly characteristic. There was so much room for improvement.

The notes of Sophie's favorite tune spilled from my mouth to her ears. A song I remembered from my early days in the hospital. My evening nurse had hummed it while she had helped me get ready for bed, tightening the straps on my wrists for my own protection.

What had worked to pacify a younger me, also worked to calm my daughter. Her wizened eyes closed with the weight of sleep. In our short time together, I had already learned the most effective technique to soothe my wee one's worries. Confidence rose with each successful attempt. Pretty soon I would be a pro.

Town was but a block away. I increased the pace of my steps while controlling the movement of my body. It wouldn't do to jostle the precious bundle I carried. To abruptly depart from the land of dreams was never a positive experience. But we were approaching the bad place, and I wanted to hurry through as quickly as possible. Getting caught up in the bad would change the course of this lovely evening, and not in a pleasant way.

Since Sophie's arrival, I had been consumed with nurturing her growing mind and body. With little time for leisure, the occasions I had ventured outside my home had drastically decreased. I had grown used to the comfort of remaining inside my domain. Gotten used to being safe with my sweet girl.

But on this frigid night we were exposed to the elements, and what was certainly worse, to the monsters who only wanted to harm me. *What if they found us? What if they hurt Sophie?*

My thoughts raced while my pace began to slow. Rather than the almost trot that had sped my body along just a moment before, heavy thoughts weighed down my pace, coating my feet in the cement of fear.

Mary Ellen, you need to stop this nonsense, right now!

I couldn't fail at being a protector this early in my daughter's life. I pushed the thoughts of their cruel faces out of my mind and focused on our goal. The brick building was finally in my line of sight.

The neon glow of the store beckoned, called out to me in my haste. The light grew larger and larger as my steps became more hurried. We were going to make it. We were going to be okay.

An electronic beep announced our stumble over the threshold. My sigh of relief echoed down scuffed linoleum aisles. Frantic heartbeats decelerated until the *thumpthumpthump* quieted from frenzied to serene.

Sophie hadn't budged during the not-quite-sprint. Her eyes were contentedly closed and her perfect lips pursed serenely together. Success was mine.

I unwrapped the scarf from my face and grabbed a basket.

"Good evening, ma'am. Is there anything I can assist you with?"

A polite voice caught my attention, and I swung around to face the inquirer. A young woman, sporting the blue vest of an employee, was waiting for me to reply.

"Oh yes, please! I do need help. My sweet girl has a cold and I'm out of milk and diapers too. . ."

I recognized the stare. Most strangers can't control their automatic response to the red scars that covered my forehead. Or the ones that ringed my eyes. Or the ones that slashed across my lips. Disgust, blended with shock, mixed with pity. *The stare.*

What had started as a helpful inquiry had rapidly deteriorated into a freak show where I was the main exhibit. I mumbled a quick thank you and darted to the back of the store. Scurried away from the helper-turned-gawker. Seems I would have to locate the items on my own, something I was used to doing.

It took twenty minutes to complete my shopping adventure. The store is quite small, but looking downward, hiding my flaws, always added time. Scanning the floor for the telltale signs of a too-close human, only gazing upward when size 7 sneakers, or size 12 boots, or size 9 flats had departed, barely breathing, not drawing attention to my visage.

Through it all, my daughter remained sleeping.

The downward cast of my eyes did have one advantage. I could gaze at Sophie's face unfettered. Absorb her exquisite profile in all of its glory. Enjoy the sight of my own flesh and blood nuzzled against a down jacket. Avoiding fellow shoppers allowed me to indulge in the sublime beauty of my girl.

The woman who had spoken upon my arrival was the employee who checked me out. It seemed as if she'd had the time to process my appearance, to come to terms with it. A slight smile marked her lips as she accepted the crinkled dollar bills from my gloved hand.

"I'm glad you found everything you needed. It's a cold one out there. Try and stay warm."

"Um, thank you. I live close by, so Sophie and I should be okay."

"How old is she?"

"Just a month. And she's the sweetest thing! Would you like to see her? I can fold the carrier down."

"A month? Oh, my goodness! I have a nephew that age, and I miss him like crazy. I'd love to see her."

The plaid fabric peeled back easily. I turned my body so the cashier could have an unobstructed view. The gasp I heard was not surprising. People always reacted with delight when they first saw my girl.

"I've been at peace since she's come into my life. I prayed for years and years, asking for a baby, yearning to hold a tiny body in my arms. And now my prayers have finally been answered." Tears welled in my eyes. "Thank you for offering to help when I came in. I'm sorry I ran off like I did. I'm not used to people being polite."

As I grabbed my bags off the counter, the cashier stuttered a reply. "Oh, yes. I'm so gl-glad that, you know, your wish came true. I'm sure th-that you're a great mom."

"I really feel like it's my true calling. There's not much else I'm qualified for, so I'm happy that I found my role in this world. You have yourself a nice night."

Curious eyes followed me out of the store. *At least she wasn't staring this time.*

Back into the chill we ventured, huddled over, quickly striding. The bad place measured twenty-five sidewalk cracks long. I knew the route well. Maintaining sight of the ground allowed me to keep track of how many concrete imperfections were passed over. Never stepping on one of course. That would be asking for bad luck.

At the halfway point, my optimism began to build. Another successful journey was well underway.

Thirteen, fourteen, fifteen. . .

My counting was interrupted by a familiar voice. I recognized the sharp tone immediately.

"Marrryy Elleennnn. Why're you out right now? Ain't it past your bedtime?"

The hard edge that marked each word shattered the burgeoning hope that had been blossoming in my chest.

"Leave me alone, Jimmy! I needed some stuff for Sophie and now I'm heading home. She's not feeling well and this cold weather is awful for her. Can't you just let me by? *Please*."

I tried to keep the pleading out of my voice, but it slipped in, nonetheless.

"You know we can't do that, Mary Ellen. You know you're in our space. Can't have our turf getting a bad rep 'cause crazy bitches like you hang around."

A ring of shoes now surrounded me. Scuffed up shoes. Footwear as neglected as the six teenagers who wore it. These boys didn't have loved ones or homes to check into. There was no one who missed them or who could keep their behavior in check when it got out of hand, like it so often did. They were alone in the world, and they took their loneliness out on whomever crossed their path. I was the unlucky person who had entered their realm tonight.

I swallowed my dread for Sophie and looked Jimmy in the eye.

"I'm not crazy! Stop saying that!"

Laughter pierced the frosty air.

"Not only are you nuts, but you're stupid, too. No matter how many times we tell you to stay away, you always come back."

A second voice chimed in. "She must like us, boys. Let's have a good time tonight. I ain't got laid in forever."

I fled. Ducked out of their circle and sprinted as fast as my legs would allow. Darted down alleys, holding Sophie to my chest, wishing for an end to this torment.

The sound of their pursuit faded as I closed in on my safe haven. A minute more and I would be beyond the gang's reach. Sixty seconds until freedom.

I rounded the final corner and fell into Jimmy's grasp. He threw me on the asphalt and advanced with menace in his eyes. "Listen, bitch, when I want to have my way with you, I'll have my way with you. Got it?"

The drops flowing down my cheeks slowed my nod down by mere microseconds. Their weight burdened my movement infinitesimally. But the delay was enough to enrage the predator.

Grabbing arms pulled the flannel carrier from my chest.

"NO! Don't do that!"

There was no hesitation in Jimmy's movements. Sophie was flung to the ground where she bounced without crying out.

"My girl! What did you do to my girl?"

Sobs made the words difficult to form. Approaching the discarded bundle was even more grueling. But I inched forward until I approached my darling and scooped her into my arms. There was a little dirt on her face, but other than that she seemed unharmed.

I looked into Jimmy's eyes, ready to battle for my family. What I saw startled me.

He was laughing. Laughing so hard he was doubled over.

"What's so funny?" I asked, voice trembling.

A few moments passed before he composed himself enough to speak. "When I called you a crazy bitch, I never knew how true it was. Until I saw you go all gaga over a fucking baby doll. Now I know you're off your rocker." The amusement left his face and his eyes hardened. "But that don't matter. A lay is a lay, so stay right there and don't give me no trouble."

While he did what he did—what he always did—my voice stumbled through the familiar strains of my girl's favorite tune. I hummed it over and over again, until the grunting was done. In the crook of my arm, Sophie slept in pure contentment.

I wasn't worried about myself. I cared only about my daughter. She was supposed to have a better life, one that wasn't blemished by the lust of others. Luckily, Jimmy didn't seem interested in Sophie at all. She was safe from this particular monster.

After he left, I counted slowly to one hundred, pacing myself, giving him enough time to leave. *Ninety-eight . . . ninety-nine . . . one hundred.*

When the last syllable exited my lips, and quiet once again settled over the area, I crawled into the entrance of my home. Toward walls that had protected me from the lurking danger in the night. Toward cardboard that had seen me through countless ordeals.

Once inside, I gently dabbed the smudge on Sophie's forehead. It came off without resistance. She was clean. Cleaner than I had been in a long time.

I placed my sleeping girl in her bed, covering her with blankets, cocooning her from the cold. The events of the evening had not permanently left their mark.

After I tucked her in, I began the nightly ritual. I had picked up three sharp pieces of glass today, and they would make for good cutting.

∞∞∞∞ ∞∞∞∞ ∞∞∞∞ ∞∞∞∞ ∞∞∞∞ ∞∞∞∞ ∞∞∞∞

Twisted Pulses, 2026

Thank you for reading Twisted Pulses. I wrote these stories over many years, and some have been published online, in audio and text formats. The poems were mostly written on Twitter during a 365-day haiku challenge I gave myself in the late 2010s.

For some reason, I forget that horror was one of my first loves. When I was a girl, I consumed movies and books drenched in blood, murders, witches, monsters, and vampires, but the first full-length novels I wrote were not horror. They're awesome, and you should read them, but it was lovely coming back to my roots and exploring the world of the macabre.

You can find more of my writing at leigh-foley.com. Thank you for your support. Without readers these words would be dead.

With love,
Leigh